ONE-WAY TICKET

By the same author

Freedman
Soldier, Sail North
The Wheel of Fortune
Last in Convoy
The Mystery of the *Gregory Kotovsky*
Contact Mr Delgado
Across the Narrow Seas
Wild Justice
On Desperate Seas
The Liberators
The Angry Island
The Last Stronghold
The Golden Reef
Find the Diamonds
The Plague Makers
Whispering Death
Three Hundred Grand
Crusader's Cross
A Real Killing
Special Delivery
The Spanish Hawk
Ten Million Dollar Cinch
The Deadly Shore
The Rodriguez Affair
The Murmansk Assignment
The Sinister Stars
Sea Fury
Watching Brief
Weed
Away With Murder
Ocean Prize
A Fortune in the Sky
Search Warrant
The Marakano Formula
Cordley's Castle
The Haunted Sea
The Petronov Plan
Feast of the Scorpion
The Honeymoon Caper
A Walking Shadow
The No-Risk Operation
Final Run
Blind Date
Something of Value
Red Exit
The Courier Job

The Rashevski Icon
The Levantine Trade
The Spayde Conspiracy
Busman's Holiday
The Antwerp Appointment
Stride
The Seven Sleepers
Lethal Orders
The Kavulu Lion
A Fatal Errand
The Stalking-Horse
Flight to the Sea
A Car for Mr Bradley
Precious Cargo
The Saigon Merchant
Life-Preserver
Dead of Winter
Come Home, Toby Brown
Homecoming
The Syrian Client
Poisoned Chalice
Where the Money Is
A Dream of Madness
Paradise in the Sun
Dangerous Enchantment
The Junk Run
Legatee
Killer
Dishonour Among Thieves
Operation Zenith
Dead Men Rise Up Never
The Spoilers
With Menaces
Devil Under the Skin
The Animal Gang
Steel
The Emperor Stone
Fat Man from Colombia
Bavarian Sunset
The Telephone Murders
Lady from Argentina
The Poison Traders
Squeaky Clean
Avenger of Blood
A Wind on the Heath

JAMES PATTINSON

ONE-WAY TICKET

ROBERT HALE · LONDON

© James Pattinson 1997
First published in Great Britain 1997

ISBN 0 7090 6025 4

Robert Hale Limited
Clerkenwell House
Clerkenwell Green
London EC1R 0HT

Photoset in North Wales by
Derek Doyle & Associates, Mold, Clwyd.
Printed in Great Britain by
St Edmundsbury Press Ltd, Bury St Edmunds, Suffolk.
Bound by WBC Book Manufacturers Limited,
Bridgend, Mid-Glamorgan.

Contents

Chapter One
MISTAKE

When Keele woke in the morning the woman was still asleep. He looked at her in the daylight that was seeping through the drawn curtains of the bedroom, and for a moment he could not even remember her name.

Then it came to him – Rona. No surname. It had been that kind of encounter – casual – in Reagan's Bar late in the evening – neither of them really drunk but a trifle under the influence. She had been alone, perched on one of those ridiculous high stools like long-stalked mushrooms, staring straight ahead at the bottles on the shelves at the back, but maybe not seeing them, absorbed in her own thoughts; and none too happy thoughts at that if he was any judge of appearances. He had been attracted immediately; and looking at her now he could still see why.

She was blonde, thirtyish, long gold hair scattered on the pillow, face turned away from him, her breathing regular and scarcely audible. Yes, she was certainly worth a second look, and maybe more – one hell of a lot more. Which was a pity in a way, because things could never work out like that; not for him; never for him.

He slid out of the bed, taking care not to disturb her, and went to the bathroom. For a while he stood under the shower, letting the tepid water cascade down his hard lean body that was, he would have guessed, not much different in age from the one with which it had been so intimately engaged a few hours earlier.

When he returned to the bedroom he saw that she was awake. She said nothing, but her gaze followed him as he walked to the window and drew back the curtains.

'Looks like being a fine day,' he said.

'What time is it?' she asked, yawning.

He turned and faced her. 'It's gone eight.'

'My God!' she said. 'Do you always get up this early?'

'Earlier as a rule.'

'Why?'

'Habit, I suppose.'

'You have work to go to? You want me out of the way?'

'There's no hurry. Take your time. I'll go and round up some breakfast while you use the bathroom. What would you like?'

'I don't eat breakfast.'

'No? Maybe you should. Some experts say it's the most important meal of the day.'

'Frankly,' she said, 'I don't give a damn what the experts say. They always get things wrong.'

He smiled. 'That sounds very cynical.'

'Maybe it's the way I feel just now.'

'Something bothering you?'

'No, not now. There was, but it's been dealt with. Nothing for you to worry about.'

She was sitting up in the bed with the duvet wrapped round her, leaving her arms and shoulders bare, and he felt half-inclined to get back in with her. But he resisted the impulse.

'Okay then. I'll leave you to it.'

*   *   *

When she joined him later in the kitchen she was wearing jeans and a roll-neck sweater and a denim jacket, which was what she had worn the previous evening. Somehow she managed to make this gear look chic, and again he could see what had attracted him to her in the first place.

'I'm going to make an omelette,' he said. 'You're sure you wouldn't like to share it?'

'Quite sure. But you go ahead.'

She watched him as he set about it. She sat astride one of the kitchen chairs, resting her arms on the back and drinking orange juice which he had taken from the refrigerator.

'Do you do all your own cooking?' she asked.

'When I'm at home. But I eat out a lot.'

'And you're a good cook?'

'The best.'

'And modest with it, too.'

It was a well-appointed kitchen; not large but with everything to hand: all the latest gadgets and nothing that was not spotlessly clean; no dirty crockery in the sink and no empty beer cans lying around. It said something about him, she thought.

The omelette was quickly cooked. Keele tipped it from the non-stick pan on to a plate and carried it to the table.

'Still sure you won't change your mind?'

'Absolutely. Though I must say it looks good.'

Later, however, she was persuaded to accept a small piece of dry toast and a cup of coffee. She nibbled at the toast and sipped the coffee, gazing at him with a speculative air.

'What,' she asked, 'do you do for a living?'

'Oh, this and that.'

'Which is as much as to say I should mind my own business. Right?'

'It's not interesting. I wouldn't want to bore you with an account of it.'

'Well, if you say so. Anyway, it must pay well enough. You don't appear to be on the breadline.'

'I get by,' Keele said.

When she was about to leave she said: 'Do we get to see each other again?'

His answer was non-committal. 'Maybe.'

It was apparent to him that she was disappointed and had perhaps been looking for rather more than this. It was as much as to say that he had no desire to carry their relationship any further.

He offered to take her in his car to wherever she wished to go, but she declined.

'That won't be necessary. I can make my own way. It's a lovely morning and I may as well take some exercise.'

He took out a wallet but she stopped him before he could open it, speaking quite sharply.

'You can put that away. I'm not a whore.'

'I never imagined you were.'

'Yet you were going to pay me.'

He saw that he had deeply offended her, and he made an attempt to mend matters.

'It wouldn't have been payment. Merely a gift.'

'I don't wish for that kind of gift. And call it what you like, it comes to the same thing.' She was carrying a leather shoulder-bag and she tapped it with her finger. 'I'm not destitute, you know. I can pay my way without help from you.'

'Don't you think you're making rather too much of this?' he said. 'I made a mistake. I'm sorry.'

'So you did think I was a whore?'

'No. That isn't what I meant.'

10

'I think it is,' she said. 'But let's forget it, shall we?'

'Yes, let's do that.'

And then she gave a sudden laugh and said with a hint of mockery: 'Incidentally, how much were you going to offer?'

He said nothing, but looked embarrassed.

'So you're not going to tell me. How disappointing. I'd be so interested to hear what value you put on my services.'

He was stung by her mockery but could see that she had a right to taunt him. The gesture with the wallet had been ill-judged and he was annoyed with himself for having made such a *faux pas*. Though he had not intended anything of the sort, it had been an insult and she had taken it as such.

But why let the incident bother him? It was of no consequence. He would never see her again once she had left the house, and that would be the end of the matter. And yet —

'I'm sorry,' he said again. 'I beg your pardon. Please forgive me.'

It was not quite what he had intended saying, but somehow the words had tumbled out; and maybe they were the right ones after all.

She put a hand on his arm and said: 'There's no need for you to feel bad about it. We all make mistakes. Nobody is infallible. And nobody's perfect.'

He saw her to the door. The house was not a large one and it was fairly old; but it had been completely renovated and he had had to pay a pretty steep price for it. Anything of the sort in that part of London was expensive. It was in a quiet street and he was on no more than nodding terms with any of the neighbours. He had never seen the interior of any of the other houses and not one of their occupants had ever set foot inside his. That was the way he wanted things to be.

He stood on the doorstep when he had said goodbye, and he watched her walking away with the late spring sunlight glinting on her hair and her heels clicking on the pavement. She turned when she reached the corner at the end of the street, and seeing him standing there she gave a wave of the hand and blew him a kiss. He waved in return and had a crazy impulse to run after her and call her back. But he did nothing, and a moment later she had turned the corner and was out of sight. The thought came into his head again that this was the last he would ever see of her, and he was surprised by the feeling of regret that he experienced; surprised because it was so unusual with him. Others had come and gone, and he had felt nothing; so why should this one have been any different from the rest?

He went back into the house and closed the door, shutting out the world but not the mental picture of the woman who had so recently left. Why? In what way was she so different from any of the others who had vanished from his mind the moment they were out of his sight? The reason was impossible to pin down; there could be no logical explanation for what he was feeling at that time: a sense of loss; there was no other word for it.

But he had to take a grip on himself, had to forget her. It was perhaps fortunate that there was no way in which he could make contact with her again, even if he wished to. And did he wish to? Of course not. There was no way he could share his life with a woman; it would not have been safe. Secrets would no longer have been secret. And for him secrecy was paramount. It was a matter of life and death.

So he would put this Rona out of his mind as completely as the others; would not even remember her name. This was what he told himself. This was what he fully intended to do.

Ten minutes later he was thinking about her again.

Chapter Two

ASSIGNMENT

He decided to go for a work-out at George's Gym. A bit of hard physical exercise might serve to clear his mind of unwelcome reflections. In any case he could think of nothing more productive to do that morning: he had no office to go to, no financial deals to make in the City. His was not that kind of business. And in fact his occupation was such that he found himself with quite extended periods when he had time on his hands and leisure to make use of as he wished.

George's Gym was a popular establishment with both men and women of a certain age who wished to achieve or retain a fair degree of physical fitness. It had all the most up-to-date equipment for exercising the muscles and working off any excess of weight. George himself had at one time been a physical training instructor in the army and no mean boxer. He had taken up prize-fighting after leaving the army but had given it up before it could do too much damage to his features or his brain. Now, at the age of forty-five or so, he was a living advertisement for the benefit to be derived from regular exercise in the gymnasium of which he was the proprietor.

His clients were all well-to-do. Nobody who was not could

have afforded the fees, which were high enough to discourage anyone of only modest means from entering the place. In this way the clientele was kept reasonably select.

When Keele entered the building he was greeted by the ex-pugilist himself.

'Morning, Mr Keele. Looks like it's going to be another fine day.'

Keele agreed that it did.

'And how's the world treating you, sir? Pretty well, I hope.'

'Well enough.'

Keele knew that George would have liked to ask a lot more questions, and would no doubt have done so if he had had any expectation of getting them answered. He rather prided himself on having a pretty intimate knowledge regarding the public and private lives of almost everyone who made use of his services. But in Keele he had come up against a brick wall; he had probed certainly, but all his probing had yielded nothing. Keele was as much a mystery to him as he was to all his other acquaintances. There were several of these but no close friends; no one who could boast of being in his confidence. They did not even know what he did for a living, though it was obvious that he was not short of a pound or two: he dressed well and drove one of the latest Jaguars.

It irked some of them, this failure to discover any but the most superficial information concerning him; a man ought to be more open about himself; he owed it to the society in which he moved. But any attempt to elicit anything more, directly or indirectly, was entirely without success. Martin Keele, they said, was a cold fish; there was something about him, and maybe it was his eyes, that warned you off; that seemed to say, this far and no farther. It could not have been more clearly stated if he had said bluntly: 'Mind your own damned business and don't poke your nose into mine.'

George was particularly niggled, because people expected

him to be able to answer all their questions regarding Keele, and he could not. The best he could do was make conjectures. He believed Keele had been in the army; he himself had served his country and he knew an army man when he saw one. Officer of course. But he had no solid evidence for this belief; it was simply the look of the man.

Keele was about five-ten in height and weighed in at around eleven stone; which meant that there was no excess flesh on him. He had a tough sinewy body and he would pump iron with a sort of contained ferocity, as though working something out of his system: a demon possibly. Yet the exercise would hardly raise a sweat in him. He was fit; there could be no doubt about that; and he could probably be as mean as they came if you got on the wrong side of him. This was George's opinion, but he took care never to put it to the test.

Keele took lunch at one of the less famous London clubs, of which he was a member. There, as at George's, he was well known by sight but had no close friends. Those who were on speaking terms discovered that conversations with him were unproductive as far as eliciting any personal details was concerned; though he appeared to be knowledgeable on a fairly wide variety of subjects. There was nothing to be learned from his accent, which was strictly neutral, betraying no discernible regional character, and beyond the confines of the club no one had the slightest idea what he did. Presumably he had ways of occupying his time, with work or play, but as to what those ways might have been he had never given the smallest hint.

Keele himself was well aware of the curiosity he aroused, and it gave him quite a bit of sardonic amusement to deny any satisfaction to the curious. He knew so much about each one of them, and they knew nothing about him except what was apparent on the surface. It was like having an advantage over all of them, and he enjoyed being in this kind of position.

In the afternoon he paid a visit to Lord's cricket ground where Middlesex were playing Hampshire. The crowd was sparse; only Tests and limited-over matches had the pulling power to fill the stands in these degenerate days. Nothing very exciting was happening on the hallowed turf, and Keele, relaxing in the pleasant sunshine, found his thoughts returning again and yet again to the woman from whom he had parted earlier in the day.

It should not have been so; he had finished with her and had to forget her, banish her image once and for ever from his mind. But he could not do it; she had a way of creeping back in. It was ridiculous, and it bothered him.

When he returned to his house in the evening there was just one message on the answerphone. It could hardly have been more terse: 'Ring A. G.'

The voice was a man's.

Keele dialled a number and a voice said: 'Yes?' It could have been the same man.

'Keele.'

'There's job come up. Are you available?'

Keele hesitated for perhaps five seconds before answering. Then he said: 'I am available.'

'Good.'

That was the extent of the conversation. Keele replaced the handset and went into the kitchen and made himself some coffee. As he sat drinking it he thought about that slight hesitation before he had admitted his availability. Had he really for a moment entertained in his mind the thought of a possible refusal? And if so, why? It was his living, was it not?

And he had never before had any doubts about accepting each assignment as it came along. So why now?

Well, he knew in his heart the answer to that, though he was reluctant to admit it even to himself. It was the woman; that woman he was finding it impossible to forget, whom he wished to see again and then again. As things were, it was out of the question, even if he could have found her. But if things were to change? What then? Maybe if he did this one last job and called it a day? Could he draw a line under the account and end it there? Then make a fresh start with the slate wiped clean.

It might be difficult; there would certainly be complications. There was one person who would be sure to raise objections because of the effect it would have on him, and he might cut up rough if services he had come to rely upon were to be abruptly withdrawn. Yet what could he do about it? Well, quite a lot if he liked to turn nasty. For he had knowledge that was hidden from the likes of George; knowledge he could use to injure one, Martin Keele, if he took it into his head to do so.

So it was not a step to be taken lightly; for there was also the question of what alternative employment was available to him. What qualifications did he have? What kind of CV could he produce to show to a prospective employer? That was a laugh. Though he did not feel much like laughing.

And all this, all these doubts and misgivings which had never troubled him before, were the result of an encounter with a woman whom he had known for less than twenty-four hours and might never see again. What was wrong with him? Was he going soft in the head? Snap out of it, Keele. Forget it.

The small padded envelope landed on his doormat two days later. It was addressed in block capitals written with a felt-tipped pen and contained just two objects – a key with a number on it and another with no number. There was no letter. There was nothing at all apart from the postmark to give a clue to where it might have come from. But for Keele the keys were enough. He had received such packages before and knew what to do.

There was a Tube station within easy walking distance of his house and on this fine day he chose to use the public transport system rather than taking the Jaguar out of the garage at the side of the house. It was not the rush hour and he had no difficulty in finding a seat on the Underground train. He came back to the surface at Euston Railway Station, and here he made his way through the milling travellers to the left-luggage lockers. With the numbered key he opened one of them and took out a black briefcase, which he carried away with him.

He did not open the briefcase until he was inside his own house. It was locked, but the second key that had come in the padded envelope fitted the lock, and when he had opened the case he saw that it contained several bundles of banknotes. This came as no surprise to Keele, for he had expected nothing less. He did not even need to count the money; he knew the exact amount: twenty thousand pounds. He was confident that it was all there.

Of more interest to him was an envelope containing some folded sheets of writing-paper. Typed at the head of one of the sheets was a man's name, and beneath it an address. There followed minute directions, and on another sheet were certain plans of a house and its surroundings. Keele studied all the details very carefully until he had the picture firmly in his mind.

The money from the briefcase he stowed in a wall-safe. There was already a considerable amount of cash in the safe, besides certain documents and a number of other objects which he considered valuable enough to warrant locking away. One of these was a Smith and Wesson thirty-eight calibre revolver with a short barrel. There were also some boxes of ammunition for the weapon and a silencer.

Chapter Three

CRAZY

The woman, whose name was Rona Wickham, was not feeling altogether happy as she walked away from Keele's house. When she had asked whether they would be seeing each other again she had hoped, and indeed expected, that she would receive a more encouraging response. His reply had in fact been little better than a direct rebuff, and she had been more hurt by it than she would have cared to admit.

Yet she would have made a guess that he had been as much attracted to her as she had been to him. Could she have misread all the signs? She did not believe so. The fact remained, however, that this man she knew only as Martin had given no indication at parting that he wished to extend their relationship.

Miss Wickham occupied a flat in Chiswick, and it was to this abode that she made her way. The flat was modest but comfortable, on the first floor of a large converted Victorian house standing well back from the tree-lined street. Having let herself in, Miss Wickham's first act was to pick up the telephone and dial a number. A woman answered the call almost immediately, and she recognised the voice.

'Oh, Jean, I'm afraid I'll be rather late coming in this morning.'

'You already are late.'

'I know. But there are reasons.'

'Is anything wrong?'

'No, nothing's wrong. That is – well, I'll tell you later.'

'So there is something?'

'Well, yes, but –'

'But you'll tell me later?'

'Yes.'

'Okay then. Be seeing you.'

Miss Wickham put down the telephone and went to the bedroom to change her clothing. She knew that Jean would want to know everything, and she wondered just how much to reveal. She and Miss Somers kept few secrets from each other. They were not only close friends but also business partners, having equal shares in a small boutique in Chelsea, which was quite a prosperous enterprise and was called the Rag-Bag. Women who bought clothes at the Rag-Bag tended to be youngish and reasonably well-heeled. Clothes there were not sky-high in price but they were not cheap either. It was a quality shop, and fashionable into the bargain.

Rona Wickham arrived at a little after eleven. She could tell that Jean was eager to hear what she had to tell, but she was not ready to confide yet; there were too many people around and there was business to attend to.

'Let's leave it for now. Have lunch with me and I'll give you the dirt.'

'So there is dirt? I can hardly wait.'

'Well, you'll jolly well have to.'

They had lunch at a small restaurant which they regularly patronised, since it was close to the boutique and served good food at reasonable prices. They had left the two girls they employed, Kimberley and Sharon, to look after the Rag-Bag while they were away, and in the course of the meal

Miss Wickham broke the news.

'Paul's gone.'

Miss Somers had a loaded fork halfway to her mouth. She checked it in mid-air. 'What did you say?'

Miss Wickham repeated the statement, though she was sure it had been heard correctly the first time.

'Paul's gone.'

Miss Somers lowered the fork untouched to her plate. 'Are you telling me he's walked out on you?'

'That's not exactly the way I would put it. We had a flaming row. Insults were exchanged; objects were thrown, some breakable. Finally I told him to get to hell out and not bother to come back because he wouldn't be welcome.'

'Oh my! That really was telling him. Good for you. And so he went?'

'What choice did he have? It's my flat and he's been living there for free, like a damned parasite.'

'Yes, that's true, I suppose. Fact is, I always did think you let him take advantage of you.'

'You never said so.'

'Would you have thanked me if I had?'

Miss Wickham gave a wry smile. 'Probably not.'

'That should have read, certainly not. You'd have told me to mind my own business.'

'Yes, I suppose I would.'

'So what was the row about?'

'Oh, you know how these things go. It started with quite a small matter; a pair of dirty underpants he'd left lying around in the bathroom. He told me I was making a fuss about nothing, and I told him he was a slovenly beast, and after that it just grew and grew. A lot of home-truths came out and had an airing, and I can tell you it was real cat-and-dog stuff, snapping and snarling like one-oh.'

'You didn't come to blows, did you?'

'No; but we were nearly there. Of course it's been building up for some time; the dirty underpants was just a trigger.'

'I thought you were in love with him.'

'I thought so too – at first. He was so charming. He could have charmed the birds out of the trees, as the saying is.''

'Well, he certainly charmed one bird. But I never liked him.'

'No, you didn't, did you? And you were dead right as things turned out. He's a bastard.'

'That's a pretty strong indictment. But if you say so.'

'I do. Of course he's been cheating on me.'

'You mean with another woman?'

'Yes.'

'You've seen her?'

'No, I haven't seen her. And I don't want to. I guessed what was happening a while ago. He denied it at first, but then he admitted it when we had this last row. Damn well threw it in my teeth.'

Miss Somers giggled. 'That must have been quite a mouthful.'

Miss Wickham giggled too. 'I suppose it does sound rather melodramatic, but you know what I mean.'

'Yes, I do. And I fully sympathise with you.'

'Anyway, even if there'd been no other woman the result would have been the same. It was inevitable really. I'd made a mistake and I just had to face the fact. Now it's finished and done with, and I'm damned glad.'

After this they got on with their lunch in silence for a while, and it was not until some minutes later that Miss Somers remarked:

'But none of this explains why you were late this morning. I mean it didn't happen today, did it?'

'Oh no. It was early yesterday evening. And then I went out and got sozzled.'

24

'Really?'

'No, not really. But I had a few drinks.'

'To drown your sorrows?'

'Far from it. To celebrate.'

'All by yourself?'

Miss Wickham hesitated, drank some wine, set the glass down and said: 'Not entirely.'

'Ah!' Miss Somers looked at her and waited for more.

'There was this man.'

'But of course. His name?'

'Martin.'

'Is that his first name or his surname?'

'First. I don't know his surname. We never exchanged them.'

'What do you know about him?'

'That he's marvellous.'

'Um!' Miss Somers appeared less than impressed. 'Am I to conclude that you slept with him?'

'Actually, yes.'

'At his place or yours?'

'His. He's got this rather nice old house in Kensal Green.'

'And when are you planning to see him again?'

'I'm not.'

'You're not? But don't you want to?'

'Yes, I do want to. Very much. But –'

'But it's not what he wants? Is that it?'

'I'm not sure. Oddly enough I had the impression that he would really have liked to arrange another meeting but that something was holding him back.'

'Like what, for instance?'

'I don't know. I just don't know. And it's all so, well, frustrating.'

'I can imagine. And what does this marvellous man do for a living?'

'He didn't say. But he doesn't appear to be short of money.'

'Did he suggest that he might get in touch with you sometime?'

'No. And he couldn't now even if he wanted to. He hasn't got my address.'

'Didn't you leave your phone number?'

'No.'

'And he didn't ask for it?'

'No, he didn't.'

'Well, he can easily find it in the book if he really wants to have a talk.'

Miss Wickham shook her head. 'He can't. You've got to remember he doesn't know my surname either.'

'Well really!' Miss Somers gave a shake of the head and appeared to be slightly exasperated. 'You know this does all seem terribly odd to me. And from what you've told me I'd be inclined to suggest that you'd be well advised to forget the whole affair. Nothing good will come of it.'

'But I can't do that.'

'Why not?'

'Because I think I'm in love with him.'

'Now that,' Miss Somers said, 'is just plain crazy.'

Crazy or not, the fact remained that Rona Wickham could not get Martin Keele out of her mind. It was an obsession. She knew that somehow or other she had to see him again.

And of course she did have one advantage that was denied to him: she knew his address even if he did not know hers.

So she could pay a call on him whenever she wished.

If she wished.

Chapter Four
BREAK-IN

In the afternoon of the day when the padded envelope had dropped on to his doormat Martin Keele took out his car and went on a reconnoitring run. The weather was still fine, and the Jaguar showed its quality by moving smoothly and quietly on its way with only the merest hint of that reserve of power which at a touch would have sent it hurtling forward at more than twice its present speed.

But Keele had time to spare and saw no point in rushing ahead like mad when there was no need to do so. He had never felt the urge to exhibit his machismo by furious driving, and he despised those who did. In his opinion they were simply revealing their lack of maturity. For him a car was not an extension of his personality; he did not regard it as a friend, nor did he ascribe to it human or even animal qualities. To him it was nothing more than a useful tool like any other, constructed from various materials for one purpose only: to transport the driver and any passengers who might accompany him from one place to another in reasonable comfort and as much safety as the congested state of the roads and the presence on them of so many idiots and maniacs would allow. He drove a Jaguar because it was an excellent car and one that he could easily afford. No other reason.

The house was situated on the north-western fringes of the Metropolis. It was a sizeable three-storey building, constructed of a greyish stone which had probably been whiter when new but had weathered gracefully. If it was not genuine Georgian it was somewhat in that style. It was the sort of house that might once have been a vicarage or a well-to-do doctor's residence: square, solid-looking, with tall sash-windows and a low parapet surrounding the roof.

It was set well back from the road and was partly obscured by trees and shrubs. A brick wall, some four feet in height, enclosed the property, and wrought iron gates on one side gave access to a gravel drive. A plate on one of the gateposts bearing the words, The Bakery, suggested a sense of humour in the owner, whose own name was Baker. It was quite certain that no bread was made there; at least not of the edible variety.

Keele stopped the car briefly to study the layout, but he remained in his seat. Mentally he was comparing what he could now see with the depiction of it that had been on the plan which had been sent to him in the post.

There was a middle-aged man in blue dungarees doing some work with a pair of shears, but no one else was visible. It looked a pleasant spot and a very desirable property which would have fetched quite a high price if it had come on to the market. But of course it was not for sale; not at present. Whether it might become available to a buyer sometime in the near future remained to be seen. Keele had a feeling that it very well might.

He put the car in motion again and drove away. Half an hour or so later the Jaguar was back in the garage and he was in his own house. It was now past five o'clock and he calculated that he had some eight hours to kill. He was perfectly calm – as always on such occasions. He was a man who did what he was paid to do without emotion. That was one reason why he was so efficient, so reliable. It was why he got the highly paid jobs. There were not many operators in his class. And yet he was completely unknown to those who used him; that was the beauty of the arrangement.

In the evening he left the house and went up to the West End. The evening was mild and Keele mingled with the crowd, unnoticed, unrecognised, inconspicuous; to all appearances a human cipher. He rubbed shoulders with hundreds, and not one of them recoiled from him in horror, as they would almost certainly have done if they had known what he was. But they did not know; that was the point. The thought brought a faint smile to his lips; a grim smile that no one noticed; or if they did made no remark upon it, since it was none of their business. In the helter-skelter and bustle of their own lives they had no time for the smile on the face of an utter stranger. He could have laughed out loud, and a few might have turned their heads for an instant; but then they would have hurried on regardless. This was London.

He had a meal; not at the club but at a small restaurant near Leicester Square. He drank nothing alcoholic and he visited no bar afterwards. This was a rule with him. Alcohol, even a small quantity, could affect one's reflexes; it dulled the senses, took the edge off one's reactions. And he had no need of the stuff; if he had had to resort to Dutch courage he would not have been the kind of operator that he was: careful, efficient and above all, effective. For this he had to be stone-cold sober and completely nerveless.

To kill more time he went to a cinema. The film held no interest for him and he dozed off for a while, knowing that he would awake in time. He was back at the house by eleven o'clock. There was nothing on the answerphone. No messages had come in during his absence. He had expected none and was not disappointed.

Later he made himself a sandwich and drank two cups of coffee. At a little after one o'clock in the morning he again left the house and took the Jaguar from the garage. He was now dressed in black trousers and a black leather jacket, zip-fastened. On his feet were supple black shoes with flexible soles and his hands were sheathed in thin close-fitting leather gloves. These also were black. In an inner pocket of the jacket was the Smith and Wesson revolver with the silencer fitted to the muzzle. The gun was loaded.

There was little traffic at that time of night, and he drove without haste along the route which he had followed earlier. He left the car in a side-street and walked the last part of the way. As he approached The Bakery he could see that the gate was closed and padlocked. But this did not bother him. Indeed, he was more bothered by the sight of a man advancing from the opposite direction. Judging by the meandering course this person was taking and the staggering way in which he was progressing, it could be guessed that he was far from sober. The light from a streetlamp revealed that he was a large heavily-built man with thinning hair and a surprisingly small head that seemed out of all proportion to his bulging shoulders.

Keele stepped aside to let him pass by, but the move was unsuccessful. A hand shot out and grabbed his arm with a remarkably powerful grip, and a pair of somewhat bulbous eyes peered into his face as if trying to bring him into focus.

'Gorra light on you?'

The words were slurred, and the breath wafting over Keele bore the strong odour of spiritous liquor.

Keele now saw that in the man's other hand was a rather mangled cigarette, which he tried without much success to steer into his mouth. He was badly off target and the cigarette came no nearer than his chin, where the impact crushed paper and tobacco into a tattered wreck which no one, drunk or sober, could have smoked.

'No, I haven't got a light,' Keele said. 'Bugger off.'

He detached the man's hand from his arm and gave him a push which sent him staggering backwards. It would have been no wonder if he had fallen, but by some miracle he retained his balance and even came back at Keele.

'Now then. No need for that.' His voice sounded drunkenly reproachful. 'I ask a shivil question and ecshpect a shivil anshwer. But no. What do I get? Bad words and a punch in the chesht. Bugger off, he shez. Why should I bugger off? You tell me that.' His tone changed suddenly from the reproachful to the belligerent. 'Now look what you've done. Made me drop my shigarette.'

He bent down, searching for the cigarette and threatening at any moment to fall flat on his face.

Keele felt frustrated. The man, by his very presence, was preventing him from getting on with his job. As long as he was there it was out of the question. And even at that hour of the night it could not be certain that no one else would come along and be accosted by the drunk. Then there would be all the makings of a scene, which was the last thing he wanted.

He decided to walk on past the gateway in the hope that the man would go on his way and leave the field clear. But when he had gone about forty yards and stopped to look back he saw to his intense annoyance that there was a dark heap in the gutter which was almost certainly the drunken man, fallen and motionless.

He retraced his steps and looked down at the heap. It was indeed the man; he was lying on his back, asleep and snoring, his stomach thrusting upward like a fleshy hill.

Keele swore briefly and thought of kicking him awake. But even if he had succeeded in rousing the man it still might have been difficult to persuade him to move on. So maybe, all things considered, the best course might be to leave him there. Let sleeping dogs lie.

Having come to this conclusion, it took Keele no more than a second or two to get himself over the wall and into the grounds of the house. Underfoot he could feel springy turf, slightly damp with dew, and he set off immediately towards the building, threading his way between the dark shrubs and ornamental trees.

Approaching closer to the house, he found himself treading on gravel. There were no lights showing in the windows, and the place was just an ill-defined mass standing under the night sky in which no moon was visible. In those typewritten details regarding The Bakery which he had received there had been an assurance that the house would not be floodlit and that there were none of those awkward lights which came on immediately an intruder went near them. It was rather surprising that a man such as Alfred Baker, who must surely have had many enemies and might have expected his property to be a prime target for burglars, should not have taken so basic a precaution. But from all accounts he was an arrogant man and maybe was contemptuous of any who might wish him harm.

Keele had never met Baker, but he knew quite a lot about him. He had a reputation in those circles in which he lived and moved and had his being. It was reputation of the darker kind, and it was no secret that the police would have liked to pin something on him if only they could have managed it. Which so far they had completely failed to do.

He had a minder, of course; which might have made him over-confident regarding his personal safety. The minder was a gorilla named Buster Jakes, who went almost everywhere with his employer and slept in a bedroom close to his. But Jakes, again according to the information supplied to Keele, was away at the moment visiting some relation in the north, and Baker had not engaged a temporary replacement – or so it was believed. On this point apparently there could not be absolute certainty. So it would be as well to be prepared.

Apart from the minder, Baker, a sixty-year-old widower, lived alone but for a middle-aged couple named Wade, who looked after the house and garden. Mrs Wade did the cooking, and the pair of them occupied quarters above the garage at the back of the house. They posed no problem.

Keele made no attempt to enter the house by any of the doors or windows. Baker might not bother with flood-lighting but it was a practical certainty that he would have a burglar alarm system installed, and there would be no profit in setting off that kind of racket. So an alternative means of entry had to be used. And this meant getting himself up on to the roof.

With no further delay Keele made his way round to the left side of the house, and with the aid of a small pocket torch he quickly discovered what he was looking for: an iron drainpipe of the stout old-fashioned type firmly attached by brackets to the wall. To a man of his agility and experience this was almost as good as having a ladder provided for his use. He put the torch away and began to climb. A few seconds later he had clambered over the parapet and was on the roof.

A skylight near the centre of the flat roof presented the climber with little difficulty in gaining access to the interior of the house. He had brought with him a small iron lever, a kind of miniature jemmy, and this made short work of forcing the catch on the skylight. A moment later he was inside.

33

He was in an attic, but his memory of the sketch of the interior that had been provided with the other information made it easy for him to find his way by the light of the pocket torch. He knew just where Baker's bedroom was situated, and having descended one flight of steep uncarpeted stairs he had only to negotiate a short passageway and he was there. He paused at the doorway, listening intently, but apart from the steady ticking of a grandfather clock in the hall below there was not a sound to be heard.

He grasped the knob of the bedroom door, turned it and pushed the door open.

Chapter Five
PROBLEM

He was surprised to find that there was a light on in the room. It was a very subdued light, provided by a red-shaded bedside lamp; but it was enough to make Keele's torch superfluous, and he put it away.

The room was large, high-ceilinged, the windows heavily curtained; which explained why he had seen none of the light showing through to the outside. There was a deep-pile carpet on the floor and some pretty solid mahogany furniture: dressing-table, wardrobes, chairs. All this Keele took in at a glance as his gaze came to rest on the bed. It was king size, big enough to have accommodated three, or at a pinch four, persons without too much crowding. At the moment, however, there was only one occupant – a man.

The man was lying on his side, his face turned away from the bedside lamp, which must have been left on when he had fallen asleep. Possibly it was his habit. Some people liked to sleep with a dim light on, having a terror of waking in the dark. All that was visible of the man was his head and one bare shoulder; the rest of him made quite a mound under the duvet, giving evidence of a fairly large body. The head was large too; cheeks rough with stubble, rolls of fat under the chin, thinning hair scattered in all directions over the wide dome of the skull, more hair on the bare shoulder, probably a thick mat of it on the chest which was not visible.

The sleeper was breathing heavily, with a kind of snort now and then, as if the air had come up against some stoppage. In sleep the man was not a pleasant sight. Awake, he might have been only marginally more attractive. There were those who had on occasion been scared stiff just by a glance from those eyes now closed in sleep. But Keele was not one of them.

He knew who the man was. He had seen photographs of him and there could be no doubt that this heavy sleeper was none other than the owner of the house. He was Alfred Baker: the mark.

Keele reached inside his jacket and pulled out the revolver, with the silencer adding length to the barrel. He could have shot Baker without waking him, but that would have been against his principles. For he did have certain principles. He always killed facing the victim, man to man, looking him straight in the eyes. It was his way.

Some people called operators like him hit-men; some called them mechanics, terminators, liquidators. He used none of these terms. In his own mind the word was eliminator; that was what he was – an eliminator.

He was a professional and good at his job; took a certain pride in it. He felt no prickings of conscience after an operation, no pangs of remorse. The men he eliminated were scum; they were no loss to humanity. And if he did not eliminate them there was little doubt that someone else would. They were already booked for that last journey which was the ultimate one-way ride. In rare moments of grim humour he had been known to refer to himself as the booking-clerk. But he never told anyone why. It was his private joke. He issued the one-way tickets for old Charon's boat.

So now he gave Baker a light tap on the head with the silencer, and it was enough. Baker woke up, turned his head and found himself staring at the wrong end of a lethal weapon.

'What in hell!' he said, and stopped.

'Curious you should mention hell,' Keele said. 'It's where you could be headed.'

Baker might have been still a bit fuddled with sleep, but he was wide enough awake to catch the drift of this. He stared at Keele, screwing up his eyes in concentration.

'I don't know you. Who are you working for?'

'Never mind,' Keele said. 'It makes no difference.'

'I'll pay you more. What are you getting for the job?'

'I don't think you need to know that.'

'Whatever it is, I'll double it.'

'And then have me killed afterwards?'

'No. I won't do that. You have my word.'

'For what it's worth. But it's no use. It's a contract.'

'So what! You're a tradesman. You can break the contract.'

Keele shook his head. 'You know that's not possible. Sorry.'

Baker started to move, making a desperate attempt to get away. It was useless. Keele shot him in the forehead; just once, because that was enough, and he saw no point in using two bullets when one would do the job just as well. The gun with the silencer on it made a dull thudding sound, and Baker, who had begun to lift himself in the bed, fell back on to the pillow.

Keele heard a faint sound behind him. He swung round quickly and noticed a door; not the one by which he had come in but in a different wall. He had glimpsed it when he had cast a glance round the room on entering, but had taken it to be just the door of a cupboard. Now he guessed that he had been wrong.

He crossed to it quickly and pulled it open to reveal an en suite bathroom, more brightly lighted than the bedroom itself. Also revealed in this brilliance was a young woman.

She was a long-haired blonde and not at all bad-looking. Her figure was pretty good too: long slim legs, curves in all the right places, nice firm breasts. All this was apparent to Keele at once, because she was wearing nothing but an expression of sheer terror; eyes wide, mouth open. Her teeth were good too.

She looked past Keele, and she was dead in line to see the bed and Baker lying on it with the hole in his head and the blood soaking into the pillow.

She opened her mouth wider and began to scream.

'Stop that,' Keele said.

No one was going to hear her except him; the Wades were too far away. But he disliked squawking females; the sound grated on his ear. And it was so purposeless. What could she hope to gain by such caterwauling?

The blonde went on screaming, whether she hoped to gain anything or not.

Keele took a couple of steps forward and gripped her right arm in his left hand. He held the revolver in front of her eyes so that she could not avoid seeing it.

'If you don't shut up I may have to make you. With this. You understand?'

She seemed to get the message and her mouth closed with a snap. She just stood there shivering, maybe with fear, maybe with cold; he could not be sure which. He lowered the gun and let go of her arm.

'What's your name?'

'Mandy Cant,' she said; and her voice was shaking too.

'What are you? Baker's girlfriend?'

'Oh no. Nothing like that.'

'Oh, I see. A business arrangement?'

'Yes.'

It was about what he might have expected. A call girl. Only she had called on the wrong night.

'What were you doing in here?'

'I was sick.'

He could believe that. Anyone who shared a bed with that lump of flesh had a right to be sick. It explained the lighted bedside lamp of course. He should have been more curious about that, should not have accepted it so unquestioningly. He had been at fault there. But his information had been faulty too; there was to have been no one but Alfred Baker himself in the house. But an arrangement like this, probably made at the last moment, could hardly have been foreseen.

Miss Cant was looking past him again at the man on the bed, 'Is he –'

'Dead? What do you think?'

'You came to do that?'

He did not bother to answer that one. It was too obvious.

'You're a problem,' he said. 'You know that, don't you?'

'I don't know what you mean,' she said.

'Do I have to spell it out? You're a witness. You've seen me. That means you're a threat to me. As long as you're alive.'

Her eyes dilated again. 'Oh no! You wouldn't.'

There was a maxim in his trade. It was: Never leave a live witness. If you did you were asking for trouble. Just one more bullet and this witness would never live to incriminate him. It would be easy.

But he had never killed a woman; he had always drawn the line at that. So was he to start now?

The blonde had shrunk away from him and she was shivering so violently now that it was a wonder she could stand on her feet.

'You wouldn't,' she said again. 'You wouldn't do it.'

39

'You're right,' he said. 'I wouldn't. I'm too damned squeamish for my own good. You're going to be left alive, and maybe one day you'll put the finger on me.'

He could see the relief written on her face. She spoke eagerly, earnestly. 'I wouldn't. Never. I promise.'

He put the gun away. 'Promises!'

There was a white towelling bathrobe hanging on the door. It was Baker's no doubt; but he would never use it again. Keele took it from the hook and threw it towards the blonde.

'You'd better put that on before you shake yourself to bits.'

She got herself into it, and it hung on her like a tent.

'What are you going to do now?'

'Well,' Keele said, 'you can be sure I'm not going to call the undertakers. My work here is done and I'll be leaving. And as soon as I'm gone I guess you'll be on the blower to the coppers.'

She was eager to reassure him. 'No, I won't do that. You can trust me. I promise.'

'There you go again,' he said. 'Promising. But it's not good enough. I have to make sure. I have to have time. So I'm afraid that means you staying in here until somebody lets you out. Maybe you can sleep in the bath.'

'Sleep! You think I can sleep after this?'

'Well, do what you like. But whatever it is, it'll have to be in here.'

'You could let me go home.'

'No, I can't take the risk. You're lucky really. You could be like our Alfred.'

'I'd have been a sight luckier if I'd never set eyes on the fat old bastard.'

'Well, that's the way it goes. You win some; you lose some.'

There was a key in the lock on the inside of the bathroom door. He took it out and transferred it to the outside.

Miss Cant watched him uneasily. 'You're going to lock me in?'

'How else could I be sure you'd stay here?'

'If I gave you my word?'

'Now you're kidding again.'

'Well, at least let me have my handbag. There's some fags in it and I need a smoke.'

'Where is it?' Keele asked.

'On the table by the bed.'

The bag was in fact not on the table; it had slipped to the floor, maybe when she had got out of bed. Which explained why he had not noticed it. He picked it up and took it to her.

'Don't look so glum. With any luck you'll be out of here in a few hours.'

'With my luck,' she said, 'it could be days.'

He left her then, closing the bathroom door and turning the key in the lock.

The drunk was still lying in the gutter when he climbed over the wall. He was snoring and showed no sign of waking. Would he remember the encounter with Keele when he did? Maybe. And maybe he would be able to give some kind of description if the police ever got round to questioning him. So, with the blonde in the bathroom, that made two. It was not her lucky night and it was not his either.

When he turned the corner into the sidestreet where he had left the Jag he discovered two skinheads trying to break into it. So that made two more witnesses. Yes, truly the luck was not with him tonight.

Maybe it was an omen. Maybe he was getting a message from somewhere that it was time to quit the game. Maybe.

Chapter Six

ME TOO

They had their heads down and did not hear him coming. His feet made very little sound on the pavement.

'What in hell do you think you're doing?' he said.

They straightened up and stared at him. They were young. In their early twenties, he would have said; possibly even younger. He guessed they were high on something – speed, crack, whatever. It could make them reckless, dangerous. As if he had not had enough aggravation already for one night!

One of them, the taller one, who had a long horse-face and bad teeth, said: 'What's it to you?'

'It's my car, damn you,' Keele said.

'So it's your car. So what?'

'You wanna make suffin' of it?' the other one asked, sneering. He was squat and pudding-faced. 'You askin' for trouble, mate?'

'I'm not your mate,' Keele said; not raising his voice, keeping everything under control. 'And I'm not asking for trouble. I'm simply asking you to beat it. Use your legs, you punks. Go.'

They just laughed.

He knew they would never go merely because he asked

them to. They were looking for trouble even if he was not. They liked it. It added spice to their lives. So he had better oblige them by giving them what they wanted.

He took the small iron jemmy from his pocket and hit the taller one on the jaw with it. He heard the cracking of bone and knew that this was one human being who would not be eating without some pain for quite a while. The man went down and did not immediately get up. He was not making any sound, so the blow had evidently dazed him if it had not knocked him completely unconscious.

' 'Ere!' the pudding-faced one said. 'You can't do that.'

'I just have,' Keele said. 'Do you want to make something of it?'

'Betcher life I do. You arst for it an' now you're gonna get it, you bastard.'

Suddenly there was a knife in the man's hand. He must have had it about him somewhere; in a sheath perhaps. He made a jab at Keele, aiming for the belly, where the blade might have sunk in up to the hilt. If Keele had remained in the same spot. But he had not. He had been ready for the thrust and he was a fast mover when danger threatened. He had had the training. So he stepped aside and struck at the man's wrist with the jemmy.

It must have jarred the bone. The pudding-faced man gave a yelp and dropped the knife. He was stooping to pick it up when Keele gave him a tap on the head with the iron and dropped him beside his pal.

They were still lying there when he got into the car and drove away.

He might have felt some satisfaction with the outcome of the encounter, but he did not. It had been yet another incident to mar the smooth execution of his assignment. It was not as he would have wished it to be.

He had of course had no misgiving regarding his ability to handle the two skinheads. To a man of his experience they had presented little threat. But he should not have had to do it; that was the point. It should not have been necessary. That they would give information to the police he very much doubted; young thugs of that description tended to steer clear of the coppers. And what information could they have given anyway? The registration number of the Jaguar? It was unlikely that they had even looked at it; even more unlikely that they would have remembered it if they had. And as for giving any useful description of his features, glimpsed only in the imperfect illumination of the street-lighting, he could dismiss that from his mind. No, they were no threat to him.

All the same, it had been an annoyance.

And once again the thought came into his head that the events of this night could be an omen; a warning to him that it was time to get out while he could before worse happened. It was superstition of course, nothing more; and he did not believe in omens. What had happened tonight was no portent of what might happen in the future. The future was a law unto itself.

Nevertheless, omen or not, maybe it was time to make a change. He had money stowed away; enough to start a business of some kind; a legitimate business with nothing crooked about it. And once again his thoughts turned to the woman named Rona. He saw her in his mind's eye and knew that he wanted to see her again in reality. So maybe after all that was the true reason why this idea of getting out of the old game now had such an attraction for him. It could be so.

He reached home and put the Jaguar away in the garage, and it occurred to him that things could have been a great deal worse if he had not come upon the skinheads before they had had time to force the door and hotwire the engine and drive the car away. That really would have put the cat among the pigeons. So there was a slice of luck for him to take into account, and he had to admit it.

It was still little more than half-past two. Much had happened since he had left the house, and it seemed to him that far more time had passed. But none of the events had taken long. He wondered whether the blonde was still in the bathroom or whether she had managed to break out. He doubted that; she would probably be in there until one of the Wades went looking for their employer and found him with a hole in the head and blood on the pillow.

Then before long the place would be crawling with cops, and they would question Miss Cant, that was certain. And what would she tell them? Everything she damn well could, no doubt. Because it was all Lombard Street to a china orange that she would not feel bound to hold anything back out of gratitude to him for sparing her life. Yet she ought to, because he had held that life in the palm of his hand, and she was a witness and the rule was that you never left a live witness. And he had left her, left her alive and kicking when he could have snuffed her out for good and all.

He let himself into the house and took the revolver from his pocket. He removed the silencer and cleaned and oiled the weapon before putting it away in the safe. Maybe he would never have cause to use it again. And maybe he would hand it in to the police if there were ever another amnesty. But no; that was just a joke; he would never go that far. For amnesty or no amnesty, it would not be safe. The revolver could link him to too many killings, and what guarantee would there be that the forensic boys would not go to work on it before it was melted down as scrap metal? Gun amnesties were a bit of a farce anyway, because the only weapons that got handed in were those that were never likely to be used for criminal purposes even if they were retained. And it was the same with knives. You could bet your bottom dollar the real villains never parted with their hardware.

Having put the gun away, he took a shower, drank a shot of whisky and went to bed. In spite of everything that had occurred he found no difficulty in dropping off to sleep, and no nightmares came to disturb his slumber.

It was the ringing of the doorbell that awakened him. For a while he ignored it. Perhaps the caller would conclude that he was not at home and would go away. But this particular caller was persistent; whoever it was on the doorstep continued ringing at intervals, until finally he got out of bed, put on a dressing-gown and slippers and went down to see who it was.

The thought was in his mind that only the police would have been as persistent as this. So had they somehow got on to him? He could not imagine how they could have done so, but somehow, somehow, perhaps they had. And if so it would not be a happy awakening for him.

When he opened the front door, however, it was not a policeman that he found standing there. It was the woman he knew only as Rona.

'You!'

'Yes, me,' she said. 'For someone who told me he got up before eight every day you took long enough to answer the door. I was about to go away. Were you in the bath?'

'No, I was in bed.'

'But it's nearly half-past twelve, for goodness' sake.'

'Is it? I had a late night.'

'Oh dear! I've come at a bad time. I'm so sorry.'

'It doesn't matter.'

She appeared hesitant, as if unsure of herself. 'Perhaps I'd better go.'

'No,' he said. It was the last thing he wanted her to do. Now that she was there, against all his expectations, he would not let her disappear again so easily. 'Won't you come in?'

She accepted the invitation at once, and they went inside. He conducted her to the sitting-room and offered a chair. She sat down, but still seemed rather on edge, he thought. He also thought she was as lovely as the picture of her he had found it impossible to banish from his mind for the past few days. Even lovelier perhaps.

She said, with a sudden rush of words: 'I know this must seem to you like an intrusion, but I just had to see you again. Maybe it was a mistake coming here. Maybe you think I'm being just one hell of a nuisance. If so, tell me straight out. I'm not going to make myself a pest, I promise you. If you want me to go, I'll go; no argument. You have only to say the word. But I've got to hear you say it.'

She stopped speaking and looked at him, waiting, as if scarcely daring to breathe, like a person charged with murder waiting for the jury's verdict.

'I don't want you to go,' Keele said.

Her face seemed to light up and the pent breath came out in a long sigh of relief. 'You mean that? You really and truly mean it?'

'I really and truly do.'

'Oh,' she said, 'I'm so glad. I'm so damned glad. You just can't imagine.'

'Maybe I can at that.'

She caught the implication of his words. 'You mean you too?'

'Me too,' he said. And he could see that he was in it now; in up to the neck. It might turn out to be one big mistake. Things might go wrong and he might live to regret this step that he was now committed to taking. But he did not care. 'Me too.'

Chapter Seven
THE PARTY'S OVER

They had lunch together at a restaurant, and over this meal they found out a little more about each other. He learned that she was Rona Wickham and owned a Chelsea boutique called the Rag-Bag in partnership with another woman named Jean Somers.

'And you're doing well?' Keele asked.

'Reasonably so. We've worked hard and built it up from very little. Now we have quite a sizeable clientele and we're getting to be known.'

Keele liked the sound of that. An attractive woman with money of her own was twice as attractive as one without a bean. And to think that he had been about to offer her some that morning when she had left his house.

She asked again the question she had put to him before. 'And what do you do for a living?'

He knew that he could not fob her off this time with the same evasive answer. But he had to step warily, because if he told her the truth and she believed him their relationship would come to an abrupt end. People tended to be prejudiced concerning those in his profession. So he temporised. He had, so he told her, been in business until recently with a man named George Smith.

'Import and export. South American trade chiefly. Six months ago we sold out to a conglomerate. George went off to the Bahamas and I've been looking round for some new venture. I've considered a few possibilities, but there's no hurry. The cash is safe where it is for the present.'

He did not tell her how much there was, but he managed to give the impression that there was plenty. She appeared to accept the story at face value and did not press him for details. He made no attempt to embroider it. Best to keep things as simple as possible. And in a way it was not so very far from the truth, except that the business he had been in had had nothing to do with import and export or with South America either.

And of course he had had no partner named George Smith; nor any partner at all, unless you could call Ambrose Gage one, and that would have been stretching things a bit. Moreover, his connection with Gage had not been broken six months ago, but was in fact not yet broken at all. Gage, so far, was quite unaware that there was to be any severance of the link between them; and when he did become aware of it Keele was pretty certain he would raise strong objections and maybe kick up quite a dust.

But none of this did he tell Miss Wickham.

And she, for her part, did not tell him about her affair with Paul Nickson. She felt that this was not the appropriate time for revelations of that kind. Later perhaps. Or, on the other hand, perhaps never.

Keele would have liked to spend the afternoon with her, but she said she had to get back to the Rag-Bag. She had taken far too long a break for lunch as it was.

'I mustn't neglect the business. It wouldn't be fair to Jean.'

Keele had some business of his own to attend to, and he did not urge her to stay longer from hers. There would be plenty of time in the days ahead for them to enjoy each other's company. They arranged to meet again that evening and went their separate ways.

From the moment when he had been awakened by the ringing of the doorbell Keele had had no opportunity to catch up with the news, either on radio or television; so he was quite in the dark regarding any developments which might have occurred in the matter of the killing of Alfred Baker. That long before this the body must have been discovered and Mandy Cant released from the bathroom was a virtual certainty. And from that the calling in of the police would have followed as inevitably as night followed day. The chances were that the body had already been examined by a pathologist and had been carted off to the mortuary.

Keele was not altogether ignorant of the procedure. He himself had on a number of occasions been the cause of the wheels of a murder inquiry being set in motion. But the hunt for the killer had never ended at his door. He had been too smart for that. He was a professional.

But would it be the same this time? In this case there had been complications, such as he had never experienced before. And the chief of these was a woman; this blonde who had the dubious distinction of being the last person to share a bed with Alfred Baker. She had not in fact seen him fire the fatal bullet, but she had undoubtedly heard the cough of the silenced revolver, and she had seen it in his hand. Most important of all, she had seen him and would remember.

And he had let her live.

It would be ironical, he reflected, if this assignment which he had already decided would be his last, should be the one that finally scuppered him.

But no; it would not turn out like that. He refused even to

contemplate the possibility. Yet in spite of this determination to cast it from his mind, that faint niggling doubt insisted on finding a way back in. Suppose this were to be his Waterloo. Suppose that streak of luck which had always been with him hitherto had finally come to an end. What then?

He bought an evening paper as soon as it came on the streets. And it was there on the front page, staring at him – the story.

There were photographs too, and one of them was of Mandy Cant, looking in reasonably good shape for someone who had spent half the night locked in a bathroom with nothing better to sustain her than a packet of cigarettes. There was one of the murder victim as well; not as Keele had last seen him with his skull smashed by a thirty-eight calibre bullet and his blood and brains on the pillow, but as he had been in life, heavily jowled and rather sinister-looking.

A third photograph was of Mrs Wade, the housekeeper, who had discovered the body of her employer when she went to take him a cup of tea in the morning. Mrs Wade was reported as saying that she had never had such a shock in all her life. Which Keele could well believe.

Miss Cant, on the other hand, finding herself in the limelight for a while and possibly enjoying the unusual experience, had seen fit to stray slightly from the plain unvarnished truth in order to lend a bit of extra colour to her story. In this Keele found himself portrayed as a terrible monster, quite an ogre in fact, who had threatened to kill her and had handled her very roughly indeed, as she had bruises to prove. It was a wonder, she said, that she was alive to tell the tale.

There was more in the report, but none of it much to the point, and Keele just skimmed through it. A detective inspector named Frank Morton had made a brief statement

on behalf of the police. It was the usual sort of thing, giving
nothing away. They would of course do their utmost to bring
the killer to justice, and they were confident that very soon
they would have more information to reveal. For the present
that was all the inspector could say, except to appeal to
anyone who might be able to help them with their inquiries to
get in touch.

Keele noted that there was no mention of the drunk or of
the skinheads, so presumably they had not come forward.
But perhaps they had not even heard about the murder as yet.
Whether or not they would feel bound to hand in their stories
when they did learn that they had been close to the scene of
the crime at about the time when it was being committed
remained to be seen. Keele was of the opinion that they
would not, but nothing was certain.

Nothing else in the paper was of any interest to him, and he
discarded it in a waste-bin and went to carry out a piece of
business which he decided was best attended to without
delay. If it was to be done at all it might as well be done at
once. In fact any postponement might lead to complications
and misunderstandings that would be far better avoided.

He travelled by Tube and his destination was in the East
End, the Plaistow area. From the Tube station he had a walk of
a quarter of a mile or so in a perfect maze of little streets until
he came to one called Harper's Lane. Halfway down the lane
he arrived at a dirty brick building which appeared to be a
warehouse. Big sliding doors were standing open and a lorry
was backed inside and was being loaded with the aid of a
fork-lift truck. Another lorry was parked in the road.

There was an office on the left-hand side of the entrance,
and there were windows in the wall nearest the door, but the
glass was so grimy that it was difficult to see through them. A
green-painted door was standing slightly ajar, and Keele
pushed it open, walked inside and kicked it shut behind him.

There was only one person in the office, and he was sitting in a swivel armchair and talking into a telephone in a rather wheezy voice that gave evidence of the smoking of too many cigarettes. When Keele walked in he swung round and stared at him as if hardly able to believe what he was seeing, breaking off in mid-sentence.

Then he said: 'Sorry. Gotta go now. Something's come up.' He slammed the telephone down and addressed Keele.

'What in hell are you doing here?'

He was a lean gaunt-featured man with a long nose and chin and lank brown hair. He was in shirt sleeves and his trousers were supported by a pair of tartan braces. The trousers were shabby and quite loose round the waist, and he seemed to have scarcely any stomach at all. There was a starved look about him, as though he were afflicted with some incurable wasting disease. Any stranger seeing him would have concluded that here was a man who would have had difficulty in finding two pennies to rub together. Those who were more knowledgeable predicted that when he eventually died – and despite all appearances they thought it might not be for quite a long time yet – he would cut up very warm indeed. Keele himself was inclined to agree with the latter view.

The man's name was Ambrose Gage.

'I came to see you,' Keele said. He had not been sure that Gage would be there, but he had taken the chance. This was Gage's place of business and it was where he was most likely to be found during working hours. 'You and I have got to have a little talk.'

'Are you out of your mind?' Gage said. 'You know you're not supposed to come here. You know we must never be seen together. That's the rule.'

'Yes, I know. And I guarantee it won't ever happen again. You have my word for that. This, Ambrose, is the last time you'll ever see me. And what's more, it's the last time you'll ever speak to me even.'

Gage's expression had become one of deep suspicion, and he was frowning. 'Now what are you getting at?'

'Putting it in plain words,' Keele said, 'it's finished.'

'What's finished, for God's sake? What are you talking about?'

'I think you know what I'm talking about. If you don't, you're dimmer than I ever thought. But you're not, are you? You're not dim at all; you're as sharp as a razor. So let's not beat about the bush any more. I've decided that enough is enough and I'm getting out.'

'Are you telling me you're not taking on any more contracts? You're walking out on me?'

'Now you're getting the message,' Keele said. 'I'm telling you just that.'

'You can't do it.'

'Give me one good reason why I can't.'

'We have an agreement.'

'Verbal. A gentlemen's agreement. But neither of us is a gentleman, Ambrose, so nothing's binding. I can get out just whenever I want to. And I want to now. Right?'

Gage took a cigarette from a packet on the desk, lit it with a match and drew smoke into his lungs as though drinking it. Keele watched him, watched the smoke come up from the depths changed in colour, saying nothing. Gage squinted at him through the haze.

'It's that tart, innit?' he said.

'What tart would that be?'

'Come off it. You know bloody well what tart. The one you locked in the bathroom.'

So Gage knew about that. Well, it stood to reason. He would have grabbed an evening paper even if he had already heard the news on the radio. As the dispatcher of the killer he had a special interest in the affair and would want to know how the operation had turned out. Gage was the middleman; he was the only one who knew the identity of both the client who put up the money and the hitman who did the job. Gage was the go-between and took a sizeable commission for his pains. Client and operator never came together; never knew who the other was. It was an insurance; safer that way.

'Now what would she have to do with it?'

'She saw you, didn't she? It's given you a fright. She could finger you. Why did you leave her alive to tell the tale? You goin' soft in your old age?'

'I don't kill women.'

Gage sneered. 'Oh dear! Got scruples, have we?'

'Maybe I have. Anyway, my decision has nothing to do with that. I'd made up my mind that this would be my last job before I even started on it.'

'Why?'

'Because I've had enough, that's why. I can please myself what I do, can't I? I don't have to ask for your permission.'

Gage looked at him sourly. 'And what about me? Don't I get any say in it?'

'Why should you?'

'Why shouldn't I? I've helped you, haven't I? I've picked up the jobs and thrown them your way. And you've done well out of the arrangement; you can't deny that.'

'I'm not denying it. But I imagine you've done well enough too. So we're quits. I don't owe you anything and you don't owe me anything. That's the bottom line.'

'And what am I expected to do now?'

'Get out of it too, or find another operator.'

'Oh yes. Easy, innit? They don't grow on trees, you know.'

'Well, it's up to you. After all, you've got the other business.' Keele jerked his thumb towards the grimy window, through which the work going on in the warehouse was dimly visible. 'Why don't you go completely legit and make an honest man of yourself? It'd be a new experience. And who knows? You might come to like it.'

Gage scowled. 'You tryin' to be funny?'

'Just a suggestion.'

'Damn your suggestions. And damn you an' all.' Gage's expression changed to one of sly insinuation. 'You could live to regret what you're doin', you know. It could turn out to be the worst decision you ever made. I'm tellin' you.'

'You wouldn't be threatening me, would you, Ambrose?'

Keele spoke softly, but he stared hard at Gage and the skinny man lacked the nerve to endure the flintiness in those eyes and shifted his own gaze away, mumbling an answer.

'All I'm sayin' is I know a lot about you, Martin.'

'And I know a lot about you. Don't forget that. It's as if we cancel each other out, you and me. Wouldn't you say that was a correct assessment of the situation?'

He was not taking the veiled threat implicit in Gage's words seriously. The man would never grass on him because in that way he would incriminate himself. But of course there were others, unconnected with the police, who might take action if they ever got a whisper regarding who it was that had dealt in so lethal a manner with their valued associates or close relations. And many of these people were the sort who would not bother with the law, but would take it into their own hands to inflict retribution: an eye for an eye, a tooth for a tooth, a life for a life.

But there again Gage would have to reveal his own hand in the business, and this would mean laying himself open to the same kind of treatment from the injured party. It would be a case of cutting off his nose to spite his face, and he would never do that, bitter as he might feel about the break-up of a profitable partnership.

There was of course an alternative way of imparting the information; the secret way that would leave his own involvement in the lethal operation unrevealed. An anonymous note dropped in a letter-box would be all that was necessary.

It was a possibility certainly, but Keele shrugged it off. He did not believe Ambrose would do anything. He would not dare to take such a spiteful and underhand action for fear the plan might miscarry, leaving the proposed victim alive and aware of what he had done.

'Look, Ambrose,' Keele said, 'why don't you just accept the situation? The party's over. When I step outside this office you'll never see me again, except it's by accident. Okay?'

Gage did not say it was okay, nor did he say it was not. In fact he said nothing at all. He just looked venomous.

Keele waited for a few moments, giving him time to speak. But when no word came from Gage's lips he turned smartly, walked out of the office, out of the warehouse and, he sincerely hoped, out of Ambrose's life for evermore.

Chapter Eight
NO ENEMIES

Miss Cant was questioned at the scene of the crime and again in the operations room, where she was invited to examine a lot of mugshots and say whether any one of them looked like the man who had locked her in the bathroom.

She had been given breakfast and she was feeling a great deal better than she had felt during her lonely vigil in the bathroom at The Bakery. She had made an attempt to open the door, but with nothing better than a nail-file from her handbag to use as an implement, she had quickly reached the conclusion that there was no hope of doing more than scratch the paint on the woodwork. She had therefore desisted and had resigned herself to waiting until someone should turn the key on the other side of the door and let her out.

She had smoked all her cigarettes before this happened, and she was all the time wretchedly aware in her mind of the gruesome object that was lying on the bed in the adjoining room. Now and then she imagined she heard faint noises coming through the panels of the door, as though someone were moving stealthily towards it; and she pictured Alfred Baker with his shattered and bleeding head sliding out from under the duvet and crawling across the carpet in an attempt to reach her. This figment of her imagination was so real to her and so nightmarish that it was all she could do to resist the urge to scream.

In the end of course it was Mrs Wade who screamed.

Dora Wade was a stout woman of stolid disposition, but the sight that met her eyes when she entered the bedroom was too much even for her self-control. The bedside lamp was still switched on and it revealed the full horror of the object lying on the pillow. So she dropped the tray she was carrying and screamed.

In spite of everything, Miss Cant had been dozing by this time, but the screams awakened her. It took her quite a few seconds to gather her wits and realise what was happening. When she did she began to hammer on the bathroom door and shout for help. By this time, however, Mrs Wade had rushed out of the bedroom to carry the terrible news to her husband and seek his help.

Arnold Wade was made of sterner material; he had at one time been employed by an undertaker and had seen many dead bodies, though never one that had been shot through the head. He was shaken by the sight of the man on the bed, but not overcome. Indeed, as he confided to his wife later, the first thought that came into his mind was that the two of them would now be out of a job and he just hoped that Mr Baker had remembered them in his will. Always supposing he had made one.

The hammering on the bathroom door and the cries for help from Miss Cant attracted his attention, and it was he who unlocked the door and let her out. He would have been more surprised to find her there if he had not seen her arrive at the house the previous evening. His mind, however, was not one of the sort that work at lightning speed, otherwise he might not have needed to ask the young lady how she came to be shut in there.

Miss Cant, having regained her freedom, was also regain-ing much of her self-possession, though she carefully avoided looking again towards the bed after casting one swift glance in that direction.

'How,' she said, with a good deal of scorn, 'do you bloody well think I came to be in there? I was locked in, wasn't I?'

'Yes, but who was it locked you in?'

'Well, for Christ's sake!' she said. 'The sodding murderer of course. Who'd you think?'

'Ah, so you saw him shoot Mr Baker?'

'No, I didn't. It was after. Look, why don't you stop asking stupid bloody questions and call the bloody coppers?'

Arnold Wade thought this might be a good idea and he went downstairs to do it, not caring to use the telephone by the bed.

By the time the police arrived Miss Cant had got herself dressed and was ready to give the full story as she knew it.

Her perusal of the mugshots led to no profitable result. None of them, she said, was at all like the man who had locked her in the bathroom. She was able to tell them, however, that he had been wearing black clothes and black leather gloves, so it would be a waste of time looking for fingerprints.

This was not the first time she had had dealings with the police, but on the previous occasions she had been treated with less consideration, since she had been under arrest for carrying on her profession in a manner not permitted by the law of the land. Now she was a star witness in a murder investigation and as a consequence was a person of some importance. She even got to see a high-ranking officer who was in overall charge of the case. This was a Detective Superintendent Reginald Milburn, an aloof middle-aged man who gave the impression of having seen and heard it all before.

Not that he did much of the questioning. Most of this was done by Detective Inspector Morton, and she rather liked him. As much anyway as she could bring herself to like any member of the Force, which she had always regarded as her natural enemy.

Morton appeared to be remarkably young for his rank, but he might have been older than he looked. He had a chubby boyish face and the sort of hair that defied all efforts with brush and comb to keep it under control. He had a pleasant manner too; not bullying like some of his kind. In different circumstances she felt that she could really have gone for him.

'So,' Morton said, going over the ground yet again, 'you were in the bathroom when the shooting occurred?'

'Yes. I told you, didn't I?'

Morton smiled, and it was a nice smile that seemed to be inviting her to bear with him because this was something that had to be done, tedious as it might seem. 'Tell me again. We want to get everything straight, don't we? And you may remember something you forgot first time round.'

'Like what?'

'I don't know. Anything. The time was somewhere around half-past one. Is that right?'

'Yes.'

'Why were you in the bathroom at that time?'

'I was feeling sick. I puked in the W.C.'

'Something you'd eaten, no doubt.'

'Maybe.'

'You say you arrived at the house in the evening. At about what time would that have been?'

'I d'know. Ten o'clock maybe.'

'How did you get there from your place?'

'By taxi. And that's another expense I don't suppose I'll ever get back now.'

Morton gave no opinion on this point. he said: 'You had an appointment?'

'Yes. He rang me and arranged it.'

'He being Mr Baker?'

'Well, of course. Who else?'

'Had he done that before?'

'Now and then. I think he liked me.'

'That's understandable,' Morton said. 'You seem to be the sort of person any man might like.'

The policewoman who was present at this interview gave him a quick, rather surprised glance when she heard this. But she said nothing.

Miss Cant accepted the compliment as no more than her due. 'I aim to please.'

'I'm sure you do. And succeed too, I have no doubt.'

'Much good pleasing him'll do me this time. He hadn't paid me, you know. Never get the money now, will I?'

'Oh, I don't know. If you put in a claim against the estate, the executors might pay you.'

Morton spoke with a straight face, and she could not tell whether he was kidding her or not. But somehow she could not see herself taking that line. She might as well say goodbye to the money here and now; put it down to experience. And what an experience! She never wanted to go through anything like that again. Though of course it could have been worse; she could have ended up in a mortuary like Alfie Baker. She shuddered to think of it.

Morton noticed the shudder. 'You cold?'

'No,' she said. Just thinking.

When they had finished with her she was given a lift back to her flat in a police car. She had ridden in this type of vehicle on other occasions, but it had always been in the opposite direction. It was another new experience and she felt like a

VIP. She did not kid herself, however, that this kind of thing would last: as soon as she was no longer of any use to the coppers they would start treating her the way they had always done in the past, like a piece of dirt.

So she had better make the most of it while she had the chance, since it was never likely to occur again.

Milburn and Morton were of the opinion that Alfred Baker's death rated as no great loss to humanity. He had been well known to the police, and had in fact spent a portion of his earlier life in jail. That had been some years ago, and since then he had prospered while managing to keep himself a step or two ahead of the law. Morton would have liked to nail him but had never been able to gather enough evidence to make an arrest. Now all chance of that had vanished; and if he ever again came up before a judge it would not be an earthly one.

'And yet,' Morton said, 'I suppose we have to do everything we can to find the killer.'

Milburn agreed. 'Murder is murder, Frank, whoever the victim is. You might figure that somebody has performed a public service in getting rid of one more villain; but it's not legal. In fact it's very illegal indeed, as you very well know.'

Morton was convinced it was a gangland killing. 'Maybe he was treading on somebody's toes and they wanted him out of the way. What do you think, sir?'

'You could be right at that. And my guess is it was a contract job. That's what's going to make it a tough nut to crack. If I'm right there'll be no motive to point us to our man. He'll be a professional.'

'So why didn't he kill the woman? You'd expect him to do that, wouldn't you? I mean to say, she got a good look at him.'

'A chink in his armour? A soft spot for the ladies?'

'And why no mask?'

'Maybe he wasn't expecting to see anyone except the

victim. He must have had information. He knew which room
to go to after he'd got through the roof.'

'But obviously his information was incomplete. He didn't
know Baker would have someone with him.'

'Well, that was a last minute thing. Like she said, he didn't
ring her up until the evening.'

'That's true.'

Later that day they pulled in Buster Jakes for questioning.
Arnold Wade had given them his name. Wade described
Jakes as chauffeur and general handyman. He did not use the
word 'minder', but Morton guessed that this was what the
man had been. Baker would have been bound to employ
someone of that description about the place, because people
like him tended to live rather risky lives. The odd thing was
that just when he was most needed Jakes happened to be
absent. But perhaps it had been known by the killer that he
would be, and possibly this had not just been an unfortunate coincidence but something that had been carefully
planned.

Immediately he set eyes on Buster Jakes the detective
inspector was convinced that he had been right in his guess
that the man was a minder. He had the look: heavy build, face
that had taken some punishment, maybe in the ring, mousy
hair beating a retreat from the forehead but long enough at
the back to be tied in a greasy ponytail, big blunt-fingered
hands. Morton would not have rated his intelligence very
highly, but he was probably ready to do any dirty job that
might be thrown his way and not ask awkward questions. He
could have been a shade over forty years of age.

Stolid though he might seem, there could be no doubt that
he was upset by the murder of his employer.

'The rotten bastard,' he said. 'Sneakin' in when I wasn't
there. I'd like to get my hands on the bleeder.'

'So why weren't you there?' Morton asked. 'I understand you've been living in the house.'

'Because there was this phone call, wasn't there?'

'What phone call would that be?'

'Woman's voice, tellin' me she's a neighbour of my ma, what's livin' on 'er ownsome up in Manchester. Says the old girl's bin took ill and is askin' for me cos she's at death's door.'

'What time was this?' Morton asked.

'Late arternoon, early evenin'; can't recall azackly. So I ask the boss if I can 'ave the time off, an' 'e says sure I can, seein' as it's an emergency like. So off I go, an' when I get there my ma's as right as rain an' she don't know of no neighbour givin' a message. No point in comin' back as late as that, so I sleep there. Get back this mornin' pretty late an' find some bastard's topped the boss.'

In fact it had been getting on for one o'clock when Jakes arrived in his car to find the police occupying the house. It had been a nasty shock to him.

Morton did wonder, however, whether it had been quite such a shock as Jakes claimed. Suppose he had been bribed to absent himself from The Bakery at that critical time. Suppose the story of the fake telephone call had been a fable. Not all minders were so utterly devoted to their employers that they were above corruption if the price was right. But on the whole he was inclined to believe Jakes.

'Can you,' he asked, 'think of anyone who would want Mr Baker dead?'

Jakes appeared to give full consideration to the question, but then he gave a shake of the head. 'No, I can't.'

'Did he have any enemies?'

'None that I know of. Very popular man, 'e was. Everybody liked 'im, an' that's the truth.'

'It appears that somebody didn't.'

'Well, I don't know who it could be.'

'You're quite sure about that?'

'Sure I'm sure. You think I wouldn't tell you if I could point you in the right direction?'

'But you can't?'

'Ain't that what I keep tellin' you? I can't.'

Morton had a feeling that Jakes was being a shade too emphatic. Baker must have had enemies, and a man as close to him as Jakes would have been bound to know who they were. For some reason he was keeping this knowledge to himself. Morton wondered why. But for the moment he let it slide.

Chapter Nine

WITNESSES

There was an artist's impression of the killer of Alfred Baker in the morning paper. It had been drawn from Miss Cant's description of the man. Keele showed it to Rona Wickham, who had spent the night at his house, much to the satisfaction of both parties.

'Do you think that looks like me?'

She inspected the drawing and said: 'Not in the least. But why should it?'

'No reason.'

If the artist's impression really was an accurate representation of the mental picture that Miss Cant retained of him, Keele could only conclude that she had a very poor memory for faces. Unless, of course, she had been deliberately misleading the man. Did she for some reason or other not wish the police to get their hands on him? In gratitude to him for sparing her life? He doubted it.

'You're not a murderer, are you?' Rona said.

Keele gave a laugh. 'Well, what do you think?'

'I think you're far too nice a person to kill anyone. Murderers are horrible people, aren't they?'

'I don't know. I've never met one.'

Which was the truth; even if he had seen one often

enough in his mirror.

'But it stands to reason, doesn't it? To take another person's life is surely the worst possible crime anyone could commit.'

Keele shook his head. 'I'm afraid I can't agree with you there. I could think of any number of far worse crimes than ending the life of a thoroughly worthless person. Some people are just not fit to live.'

'But who are you to judge which person is worthless and which is not? That would be setting yourself up as God, wouldn't it? A supreme all-powerful and totally infallible being.'

He wondered why he had started this discussion. He could see now that one thing was certain: he could never allow her to have the faintest suspicion of what he had done in the past; what he had been paid to do and had done without compunction. He had finished with it now, but the mere cessation of this activity would never be enough to expunge all that had gone before. Not in her eyes certainly. It was not as easy as that to wipe the slate clean and start afresh.

So she must never know, because the knowledge would take her from him, and he could not bear to contemplate the possibility of losing her now. In so short a time she had become an essential part of him.

It was later that morning when Milburn received an unexpected message from King Ethelbert's Hospital. It appeared that a patient there was claiming to have information that might have some bearing on the Baker murder case. It sounded highly unlikely to Milburn. The person was probably a crank. But any possibility of a lead, however slim, could not be ignored, and he sent Detective Inspector Morton along to see what this was all about.

Morton found a young man with a broken jaw lying in a bed and another young man sitting at the bedside on a chair. He noted with distaste when the nurse had conducted him to them that they were both skinheads, a type of young man he regarded with very little favour indeed. Fairly ugly ones at that.

The one with the broken jaw apparently went by the name of Chuck Warne, while the podgy one on the chair was Lennie Houlder. Morton liked the look of neither of them; he classified them in his mind as a right pair of young tearaways, but he was prepared to listen to what they had to say.

It was Houlder who did most of the talking, since Warne, with his patched-up jaw, found some difficulty in uttering the words. He was also, it appeared, in a certain amount of pain, and this made him bad-tempered and somewhat venomous.

'We bin readin' the paper,' Houlder said after the introductions had been made. 'About that there murder.'

'Of Mr Alfred Baker?'

'That's the one.'

'And?'

'We was near there las' night.'

'You mean near Mr Baker's house?'

'Yeah.'

'Is that so?' Morton said.

'Ain't that what I bin tellin' you?'

'And at what time would this have been?'

'Can't say presackly. It was late. Sort of early morning like. See what I mean?'

'What were you doing out as late as that?'

Houlder replied so promptly to this question that Morton suspected the answer had been rehearsed before his arrival.

'Bin to a party. We was walkin' 'ome.'

'You live in that area?'

'Nah. Not reely.'

71

Morton would not have believed him if he had said otherwise. It was not the kind of district a pair like this would come from. He did not believe there had been any party either, but he saw no point in making an issue of that; it was irrelevant. These two skinheads had almost certainly been wandering around looking for anything that might turn up to their advantage – like a possible mugging victim or an open downstairs window.

'Well, go on,' he said. 'You were in the vicinity of Mr Baker's house. Then what happened?'

'This geezer comes round the corner, walkin' fast.'

'What was the geezer like?'

Warne chipped in there, as if driven to it despite the pain of his fractured jaw. 'Bloody bastard!' It was a croak that seemed to come from the back of his throat.

'No doubt,' Morton said. 'But apart from that?'

'He was about average height,' Houlder said. 'All in black like. Even 'ad black gloves on 'is mitts.'

'But he was a white man?'

'Oh, yeah.'

'You saw his face?'

'Yeah.'

'Can you describe it?'

'Well, there wasn't all that much light, see? It was just an ordinary sorta face, I'd say.'

'Young?'

'No, not young. Not old, neether. See what I mean?'

'So he came round the corner fast. Then what did he do?'

'He accused us of tryin' to break into 'is soddin' car, that's what.'

'And were you?'

'No, we wasn't.' Houlder's voice rose indignantly, as though the suggestion had really shocked him.

'So what were you doing?'

'Jus' takin' a gander at it.'

'At that time of night.'

'Yeah. Ain't no law agin it, is there?'

'Then what?'

'Then 'e takes this iron bar outa 'is pocket an' 'its Chuck wiv it. Smashes 'is bleedin' jaw, like you can see.'

'Bastard!' Warne croaked.

'And then?'

'Then 'e 'its me on the conk an' knocks me aht.' Houlder fingered the back of his head tenderly. There was a bump and a small cut showing through the stubble. 'Real vicious, 'e was.'

'All this without provocation?'

'Sure.'

Morton did not believe him. The truth, as he guessed it, was that the man had surprised them trying to steal his car and had well and truly dealt with them. Obviously a professional.

He said: 'What kind of car was it?'

'A Jag.'

'Colour?'

'Green.'

'No,' Warne croaked. 'Black.'

Morton could see little help for his investigation coming from this interview. There were too many Jaguars around to identify the murderer by way of his car. These two skinheads might be of some use if it ever came to an identity parade, but first he would need a suspect, and so far he had none.

'Why didn't you report this incident to the police at once?' he asked.

Houlder looked uncomfortable. 'Well, you know 'ow it is –'

Morton did. They were not the kind who would normally

go to the police for help, being more inclined to give them a wide berth. It was the report of the murder that had changed their minds in this case. They had seen a possible way of getting their own back on the man who had handled them so roughly, and they had snatched at it. It was spite that had been the motivation.

Houlder appeared to confirm this theory. He said: 'I 'ope you catch the sod, that's all. I just 'ope you catch 'im.'

'Oh,' Morton said, 'you can count on that.'

He knew even as he was speaking that this was not the truth. There was an old saying: 'Murder will out'. It had as much basis in fact as a load of other old sayings, which was not much in his opinion. There were plenty of murderers walking the streets today as free as air; any number of unsolved killings lying in the books. You caught some; you failed to catch some. Nothing could be guaranteed.

Before he left he gave the skinheads a piece of free advice: 'Be very careful in future whose car you take a close look at in the middle of the night. There's no telling who it may belong to. And some people don't like that sort of thing, you know. They can get very upset about it. But why am I telling you this? One of you's got a broken jaw and one's got a cracked noggin to prove it. So you know, don't you?'

They did not thank him for the advice. Judging by the expressions on their faces he suspected they were not at all happy to be reminded of what the man in black had done to them. He had probably inflicted as much injury on their pride as he had on their bodies. They had thought themselves cocks-of-the-walk and had been taken down a peg or two.

As he walked away Morton was smiling. It was the savagery depicted on those two unlovely faces that amused him. He rather wished he had been present when they got their come-uppance from the man in black. He felt that it was no more than they deserved, since they were undoubtedly a brace of first-class young thugs themselves. But of course if he had been there it would never have happened. You could not have everything.

Later another witness crawled out of the woodwork.

His name was Charles Watson-Chambers, and he lived only a few streets away from the scene of the murder, which he had also read about in the paper. He genuinely had been to a party, and he gave the address where it had taken place, so that Morton could easily check up on the truth of his statement if he desired to do so.

He could not be certain of the exact time, but he knew that it was in the early hours of the morning when he was walking home and came up to the entrance to the grounds of the house known as The Bakery. There, according to his account, he had been brutally attacked by a man who had approached from the opposite direction. This man had punched him so hard on the jaw that he had been knocked unconscious and had only come to his senses some time later to find himself lying in the gutter and the attacker nowhere to be seen. He knew now, of course, that the man had gone into the house to murder Mr Baker. He felt that he was extremely lucky himself to be alive to tell the tale.

Morton had strong doubts about the complete accuracy of this story. He had a feeling that Mr Watson-Chambers was embroidering it to some extent. For why would a hit-man going about his business launch an unprovoked attack on an innocent passer-by? It just did not make sense.

He looked at Watson-Chambers and could see no bruise on his chin, and a blow such as the man had described would surely have left some mark. What he did see was a plump mottled face, with watery eyes and a bulbous nose, the colour of which gave ample evidence of having been stoked up by many years of hard drinking. His guess was that Watson-Chambers, returning from the party at a late hour, would have been in no condition to retain a very accurate picture of what had subsequently taken place on the night in question.

Nevertheless, he invited this dubious witness to give a description of the man who had allegedly attacked him.

'He was very big,' Watson-Chambers said. 'Absolute giant of a man. Rude too. Told me to bugger off. Damned insolence. I remonstrated with him, and that was when he hit me.'

'Yes, but did you get a good look at his face?'

'Of course. It was an ugly one. Bruiser type. Ex-prizefighter, I shouldn't wonder.'

'Any special features?'

Watson-Chambers appeared to give this question some thought and finally came up with a scar. 'On the right cheek. No, the left.'

Morton came to the conclusion that he could ignore this information. The witness's vision had probably been pretty blurred at the time, and he had no doubt thrown the scar in to lend colour to the story. When he came to describing what his attacker had been wearing he seemed to be on firmer ground.

'Black. All in black. In keeping with his character, wouldn't you say, Inspector?'

Morton said nothing. He simply reflected that this was the one point on which all four witnesses agreed: that the man had been wearing black. And a fat lot of use that was going to be in running him to earth.

Chapter Ten

THE BAKER BOYS

The Baker Boys were relaxing with their girlfriends in the sunshine of the Costa Brava when the news reached them. They packed their bags at once and flew home, leaving the girls in the villa in Spain with strict instructions to stay where they were until they received orders to do otherwise.

Barney and Maurice were the late Alfred Baker's sons, and they were generally known around and about in the circles in which they moved as the Baker Boys. They were also called a lot of less complimentary names by a considerable number of those with whom they did business, and who had very good reason to dislike them and even to wish they were dead. But these names were never used in their presence because they might have taken offence, and when they took offence they were inclined to become very violent indeed.

They were, of course, only following in their father's footsteps, and those who disliked them invariably detested their father also. And feared him.

They were not really boys. Barney was thirty-six and Maurice was thirty. They were not much like each other in appearance, Barney being ginger-haired, round-faced and freckled, while Maurice had black curly hair and a dark complexion. The rumour was that Maurice was not in fact Alfred's son at all, but had been fathered by a handsome Italian waiter, who disappeared in mysterious circumstances long before the child was born. This rumour was never mentioned in Alfred's presence, because it would not have been a healthy thing to do. He would have resented it quite bitterly and would almost certainly have taken strong action to wipe out the slur. All the more so because he certainly knew that it was true.

Mrs Baker had died when Maurice was only five. She had no other children after him. Following her death Alfred had taken on the responsibility of bringing up the boys, and it was often remarked upon that he had never treated the younger boy any differently from the older. There had been no favouritism that might have set one against the other, and there had always been a strong bond between the two, as well as between them and their father.

Now, in the hour of tragedy, they felt the blow with equal force. Their sorrow at the bereavement was matched only by the intensity of their rage and the bitter anger directed at the unknown killer. When the immediate shock had passed they were possessed by a burning desire for vengeance, and it made of them two very dangerous young men.

Detective Inspector Morton had an interview with the brothers at the first opportunity after their return to London. It took place at The Bakery, where they were trying to get a few things sorted out now that their father was dead. The body had been taken away and the police were no longer there in force; but the Wades and Buster Jakes were still in the house. Barney and Maurice had already had a talk with all of these and now had an outline of what had happened.

The Wades could tell only of how they had found the murdered man lying on the bed and the young woman locked in the bathroom. It was obvious that they were worried about the prospect of losing their jobs, but they were given no reassurance in this respect. It seemed certain that the house would eventually be sold, and they could only hope that the new owner would take them on. Of this there could be no guarantee and the future looked bleak.

The brothers had a private talk with Jakes. Naturally they wanted to know why he had not been on hand when he was most needed.

'You were his minder, weren't you?' Barney said. 'So why in hell weren't you doing your job?'

Jakes looked uneasy. He had foreseen that he would be blamed for not being on duty at the crucial time; and all he could produce in his own defence was the story of how he had been lured away by a false telephone call telling him his mother was desperately ill and was asking for him. Even as he was telling it he was aware of the feebleness of it as an excuse, and he could see by the expressions on the brothers' faces that they were not buying it. In fact they were highly suspicious.

'You fell for that?' Maurice said. 'You're asking us to believe you're that dumb?'

'It sounded genuine. How was I to know it wasn't kosher?'

'How do we know what you're telling us is kosher either?' Barney said. He gave Jakes a searching look which made the big man squirm. 'Have you been got at, Buster?'

'Got at? Don't know wotcher mean.'

'I mean did somebody slip you a backhander to make yourself scarce while this joker slipped in to do the business? Is that the way it was?'

Jakes looked pained. 'As God's my witness. I never took no backhander. You know me, Barney.' He turned to the other brother. 'And you know me too, Maurie. Would I do the dirty on your old dad, what I loved like he was my own father? Now I ask you, would I do a thing like that, whatever I was offered? Think about it. Would I?'

They thought about it and came to the conclusion that Jakes was telling the truth. It was doubtful indeed whether anyone would have tried to bribe him, since it was well known that he was devoted to Alfred Baker and would have gone straight to his employer to warn him of the plot.

The fact remained, however, that someone had lured Jakes away from his bodyguard duty so that the killer could do his work unhindered. And it had to be someone who knew the arrangements of the household at The Bakery pretty accurately. So who would have been the possessor of this knowledge and would also have wished to remove Alfred Baker from the land of the living?

'The Rackerman mob,' Barney said. 'Who else?'

Maurice agreed. 'I'd say you're dead right. It stands to reason.'

And Jakes was of the same opinion. 'It's what I figured too.'

Barney said quickly: 'You didn't tell the coppers that?'

'Leave it out,' Jakes said. 'I may be thick, but I ain't that thick. I wouldn't tell them nothing, except I had the say-so from you. I just said as I didn't know nobody what could've wanted Mr Baker dead because everybody liked him.'

'Good,' Barney said. 'This is something we handle ourselves. Don't want the boys in blue shoving their oar in.'

Jakes nodded. 'Thought you wouldn't.'

Jesse Rackerman had at one time been Alfred Baker's partner in crime and had spent much time at The Bakery, playing cards or snooker or just sitting around and talking. Then there had been a falling-out over a woman they both had their eyes on, and Rackerman had gone off in a huff and formed his own gang.

The real trouble started when they began treading on one another's toes. Both gangs were in the protection racket, and their territories were too close together for comfort, because each lot wanted to expand at the expense of the other.

Rackerman, a stringy hawk-faced man with a slight squint, was younger than Baker and perhaps rather more ambitious. He suggested that it was time for his former partner to retire. On his ill-gotten riches he could comfortably afford to do so and maybe take off for some safe haven in the sun. Moreover he, Rackerman, was willing to pay quite a handsome sum in return for the extra business that would be his when the deal was completed.

He did not state any exact figure for the sum he was prepared to hand over for the business, which included other activities besides the protection racket, and it never came to the point because before he could go any further Alfred Baker said bluntly:

'Over my dead body.'

At times Rackerman's features were capable of taking on an expression which could only be described as thoroughly evil. At these times he could well have been used as a model for a painting of the devil himself. This was one such time.

'If that's the way you want it,' he said, 'so be it.'

Without another word he got up and left.

Alfred Baker was destined never to see him again.

Baker had never mentioned Rackerman's ominous parting words to anyone. Therefore his sons knew nothing of this implicit threat to his life. Had they been aware of it, they would have been even more certain that Rackerman was behind the killing. Even as it was, his was the name that came immediately into their minds when guessing who had arranged it. They did not think for a moment that he had carried out the operation himself; he would most certainly have employed someone else to do the dirty work. But he had wanted Baker out of the way; of that there could be no doubt. And he might have figured that with the head of the family disposed of it would be easy to do a deal with the sons in the matter of handing over territory.

If so, in this he had seriously misjudged the two with whom he would now have to bargain. If he thought they would be intimidated by the murder of their father he had made a very grave mistake indeed.

That there were many other people who would weep no tears at the departure of Alfred Baker for fresh woods and pastures new in some other world, and indeed could have wished for no better dispensation, was certain. These were people he had battened on, extracting a toll for the privilege of having him protect their businesses. Some had resisted this imposition, refusing to pay up, and unpleasant things had happened to them; a brick hurled through a shop window might have been the least of these, a disastrous fire destroying uninsured stores, the worst. Most people paid up and avoided such catastrophes – at a price.

But although all these would read of Alfred Baker's demise with joy in their hearts, tempered perhaps by the reflection that there were others waiting in the wings to take over his part now that he had gone, it was unlikely that any of them would have had the courage to carry out the killing. They were just small businessmen, law-abiding, industrious and reasonably prosperous, almost certainly resentful of the toll levied illegally upon them but not prepared to take such drastic action to rid themselves of the incubus that had battened upon them.

So it had to be Rackerman who had engineered the death; of this the brothers were convinced. And it was he who must be made to pay for the death of their father; on that point they were of one mind.

And Buster Jakes agreed with them.

Morton got very little help from the Baker Boys. Like Jakes before them, they said they could think of no one who might have borne a grudge against their father and would have wanted him dead.

'You're sure of that?'

'Oh yes,' Barney said. 'We've been trying to think of someone, but nothing's come up. We'd like to help you, Inspector, you know that. After all, we're as keen as anybody to have the bastard that killed our dad brought to justice, ain't we, Maurie?'

'That's right,' Maurice said. 'There's someone out there what pulled the trigger on him, and we want the bugger nailed for it.'

'Has it occurred to you,' Morton said, 'that it may have been a contract killing?'

'Is that what you think it was?'

'Let's just say it's a possibility that should be borne in mind when looking for the murderer.'

'So you're suggesting that somebody could have hired the swine to do the killing.'

'It happens,' Morton said. And he knew there was no need to tell them that. They knew all about the way these things were handled in the underworld, because they themselves were of that culture. They had grown up in it. They were, in a word, villains; and it was very unlikely that anything they said to him would be the truth, since it would be second nature to them to lie to the police. 'Yes, it does happen.'

'But who,' Barney said, 'would want to take out a contract on our poor old dad, who never did nobody no harm?'

He said this with such a straight face and so much of an appearance of utter sincerity, as though he really believed in every word he was saying, that Morton could not help reflecting that he would have made an excellent actor. The very idea of Alfred Baker's never having done harm to anyone was so bizarre that it was quite laughable.

Morton did not laugh or even smile. He said: 'A business rival, perhaps?'

'Someone in the car trade, you mean?'

This was not what Morton had meant, and he knew that the brothers were well aware of it. There was an establishment down Stratford way which traded under the name of Aybee Motors. It was a front for the other business, which brought in the real money.

'It's not impossible, is it?'

Barney seemed to give it some thought before shaking his head. 'Nah. It's a cutthroat business, sure enough, but we don't go round topping our rivals. That'd be taking things a bit too far.'

'Somebody took it that far with Mr Baker.'

'You don't have to remind us. So what are you doing about it?'

'We're doing all we can. We're not just sitting on our behinds waiting for something to turn up. But there's not a lot to go on. We were hoping you could give us a lead.'

'Well, we can't and that's that.'

Before he left Morton gave a word of warning. 'I hope you're not thinking of taking the law into your own hands on this.'

'What makes you think we might?' Barney asked.

'Just an idea that happened to cross my mind.'

'It's the wrong idea. We wouldn't never do a thing like that. Meanter say, it's your job, not ours.'

'Exactly,' Morton said. 'And I hope you'll remember that.'

'Oh, sure we will,' Barney said. And Morton had the feeling that the man was mocking him. Which he did not care for at all. 'Won't we, Maurie?'

'Of course,' Maurice said. 'We're always careful to remember any piece of advice given us by the police.'

Morton went away with the firm impression that the Baker Boys were a pair of cocky villains who knew a lot more than they were admitting. Some day he hoped to slip the handcuffs on them, but for the present he had to bide his time.

Chapter Eleven
NO REGRETS

Rona Wickham had moved in with Keele, though she had not for the present given up her flat. She hesitated to take that step, feeling that it might be tempting fate. That this was sheer superstition she knew very well, but she could not dismiss the feeling that if she cut herself off from this line of retreat things might go wrong and she might live to regret it.

Not that things showed any evidence of going wrong. She and Martin could never have too much of each other's company. When they had been living together for nearly a week she asked him whether he had any misgivings regarding their relationship.

'Do you ever wish you'd never met me?'

'What a stupid question,' he said. 'You must know it was by far the best thing that could have happened from my point of view.'

'So you still love me?'

'In less than a week,' he said, 'would you have expected me to fall out of love?'

'I can't say what I expected. I just know what I hoped.'

'And that was?'

'That you would love me for ever.'

'I'll make you a promise,' he said, 'that I'll love you as long as you love me.'

She gave a laugh. 'Then it will be for ever.'

He would have liked to believe it; but he was too much of a realist not to have doubts. For the present all was fine, and they were entirely bound up with each other; but time brought changes, inevitably; nothing remained the same. And so it might be with them, for why should they be in any way exceptional? But why dwell on that? The only sensible course was to take what the moment offered and not plague oneself with fears that it might not last.

'I cannot even begin to imagine a time when I might stop being in love with you,' she said.

For his part, he could imagine it very well; but he did not say so. He knew that the only question was: which of them would first tire of the other? For that this would happen sooner or later was a virtual certainty. After all, they were only human.

She had taken him to the Rag-Bag and had introduced him to Jean Somers. Later Miss Somers had given her opinion of him.

'He's quite handsome, of course. I can understand your falling for him. It wouldn't be difficult for any woman to do that. But he doesn't have a lot to say for himself, does he?'

'If you mean he isn't a chatterbox, that's true. But he talks to me.'

'Well, I suppose he would, wouldn't he? But how much do you really know about him?'

'Enough.'

'Which, I imagine, is one way of saying, not a great deal. I get the impression that there are hidden depths to him. Perhaps he has some dark secrets he wouldn't want the rest of us to know.'

Miss Somers spoke lightly, but her partner detected rather more than mere banter in the words: possibly a warning to her not to become too involved. But of course she was already involved and had no wish not to be. And even though it might be true that she did not yet know much about Martin's background, she felt certain that everything would be revealed as time passed, and that there would be no skeletons in that cupboard.

'You are not, I suppose, thinking of marrying him?'

'The question of marriage hasn't even been mentioned. After all, it's a trifle early for that, isn't it?'

'Well, don't be in too much of a hurry. It may turn out fine, and I hope it does for your sake. But you never can tell, can you? Things have a way of going wrong.'

Miss Wickham thought this was striking an unpleasantly pessimistic note. But of course Jean herself had had an unfortunate affair with an all too plausible charmer, and this had made her rather cynical where men were concerned. So she refused to let herself be discouraged by these remarks. She was convinced that there would not turn out to be anything disreputable about Martin. She could not have fallen so deeply in love with him if it had been otherwise. It did not even occur to her that this was a non sequitur; that there was no logic in it. But when had logic ever been a factor in such matters?

Keele's opinion of Miss Somers was that she appeared to be a capable and sensible kind of person.

'I don't think she cared much for me, though.'

'Now what makes you say that?'

'I got the impression that she was suspicious of me. I don't blame her. To her I must appear like some predator aiming to get his fingers on a slice of her partner's hard-earned money.'

'But that's ridiculous.'

'Of course it is. You know it and I know it. But she's seeing the thing from a different viewpoint.'

'I'm sure you're wrong. But let's not argue about it.'

'I'm not arguing,' Keele said. 'After all, it makes no difference to us what she thinks, does it?'

Rona agreed. Nevertheless, she would have preferred to have had Miss Somers's wholehearted approval of her most recent attachment without those rather depressing reservations.

Keele had been keeping an eye on the papers and reading accounts of progress in the Baker murder investigation. In fact, there appeared to be very little progress to report, and as usual with such matters interest waned and the subject tended to drop out of the news columns.

No arrest had yet been made, and apparently no suspect had been brought in for questioning. So there was nothing for the great British reading public to get its teeth into. The story of the blonde in the bathroom discovered completely nude by the killer had had a mildly salacious flavour to it that had aroused initial interest, but this could not last and new subjects of greater moment had thrust it into the background.

Keele was pleased. It was obvious that the evidence of Miss Cant, the drunk and the two skinheads had been insufficient to turn the eyes of the investigating officers in his direction. Which was no more than he had expected. His great advantage was that he was quite unknown to the police and appeared nowhere in their files. Moreover, he had never had any connection with the murdered man and therefore could have had no motive for killing him. In fact, there was only one person who could have pointed the finger at him, and that was Ambrose Gage. And however resentful Gage might feel at his abrupt severing of their business relationship, he still did not believe that the man would seriously contemplate turning him in. The risk to himself would have been too great.

So he felt that he could relax and give himself over entirely to this new and altogether delightful way of life in the company of the charming Miss Rona Wickham.

Those of his acquaintance at the club and elsewhere who believed that Keele had been in the army were in fact correct in their thinking. He had at one time served with that élite body of men known as the SAS. With them he had learned those arts of combat so useful to the fighting man and of so limited a use to the ordinary law-abiding citizen. Among these arts was that of killing.

But he had never really fitted in. He had been educated at a public school, and his father had been a major in the army until forced to take early retirement. Keele was the black sheep of the family and had had nothing to do with any of his relations for years. He doubted whether any of them knew if he was alive or dead; or cared either. And that was just the way he wanted it.

His father had not approved at all of a son of his enlisting in the army as what Kipling would have called a gentleman ranker. But he didn't give a damn for his father's opinion. Nor did he give a damn if he never saw the stuck-up old bastard ever again.

He had left the SAS under something of a cloud, as the result of an incident in which he had been involved. The affair had taken place in Northern Ireland, and there was a woman concerned in it. There had been some kind of duel between Keele and another man, with knives, and the other man had been fairly severely wounded. For reasons of security the matter had been hushed up and it had never come to a court-martial. But he had found himself discharged from the army. Without honour.

In the first few years following his discharge he moved from one poorly-paid job to another. He had undoubted skills, but they were not of a kind to appear attractive to a prospective employer when presented on a CV. He had the attributes of being strong and healthy, and he worked as a labourer on building-sites and on road construction and in warehouses; but he wanted something better, something that would bring in real money.

Then he met Ambrose Gage.

It was in a public house in Bermondsey. They happened to rub shoulders and Gage started talking. Before long he had made himself acquainted with Keele's history. Keele, normally reticent, had on this occasion allowed his tongue to be loosened under the influence of the drinks that Gage was paying for. So he succumbed to the skilful probing of this skinny stranger and related to him stories about himself that he had never told to anyone else.

'So,' Gage said, 'you have killed people?'

'Yes,' Keele said.

'And no regrets?'

'Why should I have any regrets? It was part of the job.'

'And you would do it again?'

'If necessary.'

Gage drank some beer, put the glass down, turned his beady little eyes on Keele and said:

'How would you like to earn yourself a lot of money?'

'Show me the way,' Keele said. 'Just show me the way.'

He still had no regrets. But it was finished now, and he would never go back to it. That chapter of his life was concluded and a new one had begun. The two had to be completely separate; nothing from the one must be allowed to spill over into the other, because that might ruin everything. Unless something quite unforeseen occurred he felt sure that nothing would.

Chapter Twelve
PROPOSAL

Jesse Rackerman rang up Barney Baker at eleven-thirty in the morning.

The call came as no surprise, because the brothers had been expecting a feeler from that quarter and were beginning to wonder what was holding Rackerman back. Perhaps he was giving them time to come to terms with the loss of their father. If so, it was out of character with him to be so considerate.

'What do you want?' Barney demanded. Though he could have made a pretty shrewd guess at the answer. He put a hand over the mouthpiece and spoke to his brother, who was with him. 'It's him. Rackerman.'

Maurice nodded. 'At last.'

'I thought we ought to have a little get-together,' Rackerman said. 'You and Maurie and me. What d'you say?'

'What for?'

'For a discussion, that's what.'

'Do we have anything to discuss?'

'Well, sure we do, Barney. Business, my friend, business.'

'What business would we have to discuss with you?'

'What business! Why, yours, of course.'

'I didn't know you were that interested in the used car trade.'

Jesse Rackerman gave a throaty chuckle. 'You will have your little joke. Used cars! That's rich, that is. But you and me, we know that's not what we're talking about. I had a natter with your old dad about it, but before we could do a deal he got hisself rubbed out. Such a shame! Such a loss to society! But that's the way it goes. Here today and pushing up the daisies tomorrow. So now it looks like it's his boys we have to deal with.'

'And suppose his boys don't want to do a deal?'

Rackerman gave another chuckle. 'So you're going to play hard-to-get? Well, okay. But where's the harm in a friendly powwow? Won't lose you nothing to talk.'

Barney answered, as though turning the question over in his mind: 'Oh well, maybe not. So why don't you come along to our place and we'll kick it around a bit.'

As he had expected, Rackerman was not at all in favour of this suggestion.

'No, I don't think that would be a good idea at all. You come along with Maurie to see us and we'll make you an offer. If you like it, well and good. If not, no bones broke. What you say?'

Barney hesitated, though the hesitation was a sham, since he and his brother had anticipated all this with dead accuracy and knew just what they would do. So he said:

'Okay, then. Why not make it this evening? That suit you?'

'Fine,' Rackerman said.

'It'll have to be late. We got things to do. How about eleven o'clock, if it's not past your bedtime?'

Rackerman gave another of his throaty chuckles. He seemed to be enjoying himself. 'For a meeting with you boys I'd sit up all bloody night.'

'Good. Now let's get this clear. We're talking about your place of business, ain't we? Not your private house.'

'That's right. I never do business at home. It's a rule.'

'Thought so. We'll be seeing you then.'

Barney put the telephone down and said: 'We've got him. We've got the bastard and he just don't know it. He thinks he's got us. He's got a nasty surprise coming to him.'

'Not before time neether,' Maurice said.

Rackerman's place of business was south of the river in the Wandsworth area. Like Aybee Motors, it was just a front for other activities. There was a single-storey brick building that had once been a laundry, and there was a tarmacked yard that went with it. From this base Rackerman ran a small transport business with a few lorries and vans which seemed to spend much of their time out of action, parked on the tarmac and waiting for the call.

Access was by way of a narrow lane, and when the Baker Boys arrived just before eleven there was scarcely a sign of life anywhere around. Maurice had been driving, and he stopped the BMW alongside a blue Transit van. He and Barney got out and walked towards the end of the big building, where an office now occupied what had formerly been the laundry manager's quarters.

There was a light above the door and Barney gave a knock with his knuckles. The door was opened within seconds, and Rackerman himself was standing there to welcome them in.

'Dead on time,' he said. 'Dead on time.'

Maurice thought it was a rather ominous expression to use. It could have a double meaning.

Rackerman squinted at them and then past them, as if making sure there was no one else lurking in the background. Then he stood aside to let them into the rather cramped lobby before closing the door. He did not lock it but led the way into a fair-sized room, which might have been used for taking meals in earlier in its existence. There was a rectangular oak table in the centre, with a number of upright chairs ranged along the sides.

There were three men already in the room, all standing on the far side of the table. The Baker Boys recognised one of them at once; he was Rackerman's cousin, a man named Swan. He wore glasses and there was a studious look about him, which made him the odd one out in that group. He was so slightly built it might have been thought that a strong wind would have blown him away; but he had the reputation of being a wizard with figures and was a treasure to Rackerman in keeping the books looking all above board.

The other two were heavies. They looked tough and they looked as though they knew it. It was not, however, their toughness that bothered the Baker Boys; it was the fact that one of them was holding a big black automatic pistol in his fist, and it was pointing straight at them.

'Now what in hell is this?' Barney demanded. 'What's the gorilla got the shooter in his mitt for?'

Rackerman had quickly moved himself away from the brothers so that he would not be in the line of fire. He said:

'Just a precaution. Tommy isn't going to shoot you.'

'I'm glad to hear it,' Barney said. 'But I wish he'd point that gun in some other direction. Preferably at himself.'

'All in good time,' Rackerman said. He made a sign to the other heavy. 'Now, Dod; get on with it.'

The one called Dod walked round the end of the table and came up behind the brothers. He frisked one and then the other. He found a gun on each of them – a revolver on Barney and a Walther self-loader on Maurice. He carried the weapons away and placed them on the mantelpiece above the old-fashioned fireplace, with the table between them and their owners.

Rackerman shook his head reprovingly. 'I'm surprised at

you two, coming armed. Don't you trust us?'

'Seems like you don't trust us,' Barney said. He spoke disgustedly, like a man who has been outmanoeuvred and is not at all happy about it. 'I should've known.'

'We all make mistakes,' Rackerman said. 'No harm done. Now let's just sit down and have our little talk, should we?'

He himself moved to a chair at one end of the table and sat down. Swan took a chair close to him. The Baker Boys, now disarmed, sat down on the side of the table nearest the door, which was behind them. They looked disgruntled but resigned to the situation. The two heavies remained standing, but Tommy had put the gun away.

'Now,' Rackerman said, 'let's get down to business. I imagine you boys have guessed what this is all about.'

'You made it pretty clear on the blower,' Barney said. 'But maybe you'd better spell it out so's we've got it all straight.'

'Sure. Basically it's this – we'd like to take over your manor. For a consideration of course.'

'That's what I thought. And it's what you were proposing to our dad, wasn't it?'

'So it was.'

'And I reckon he told you what you could do with your offer, didn't he?'

'Well,' Rackerman said, 'I must admit he wasn't very receptive. But what the hell! He was an old man and set in his ways. Now he's gone and it's a whole new ball game. Of course I was shocked to hear of his death, very shocked indeed.'

'Oh, for Christ's sake!' Maurice said. 'Spare us the crocodile tears. We can do without them.'

Rackerman grinned wolfishly. 'Always down to earth, our Maurie. You was like that even when you was a kid, as I recall. And incidentally,' he said, as if suddenly noticing something, 'I see you didn't bring Buster along with you.'

'Why should we? He was the old man's minder, not ours.'

'And didn't mind him all that well, so it seems.'

'He was away at the time,' Barney said.

'Is that so? Well, that's the way it goes – you have a minder and when you really need him he's nowhere around.'

'He was called away. Somebody handed him a duff message on the blower that his dear old ma up in Manchester was at death's door.' Barney looked hard at Rackerman. 'Of course you wouldn't know nothing about that?'

'Me?' Rackerman played the innocent wrongly accused. 'What would I know about it?'

Maurice broke in impatiently: 'Look, where's this getting us? Why don't you tell us what your proposal is, so we can be on our way. We've wasted enough time as it is.'

'There speaks the voice of reason,' Rackerman said. He turned to Swan. 'Show them, Harry.'

Swan reached under the table and came up with a black briefcase. He put it on the table and released the catches. When he raised the lid it was revealed that the inside was stuffed with bundles of banknotes.

'There,' Rackerman said. 'That's what we're offering for your business. And I'm not talking about old cars neither.'

'How much is in there?' Barney asked.

'Twenty-five grand.'

Barney gave a derisive laugh. 'You must be joking.'

'You think it ain't enough?'

'Even if we was thinking of selling, which we ain't, this wouldn't be near enough. We know it and you know it. So what's the game, Jesse?'

'You think it's a game?'

'It's gotta be. Stands to reason. You can't believe we'd hand it all over to you for a piffling twenty-five gees.'

Rackerman said softly: 'If you know what's good for you, you might just do that.'

'Are you threatening us?' Maurice asked.

'Threatening you? Why no, not at all. I'm just giving you a health warning. Your pa didn't look after his health too good, and see where it got him. In the dead meat shop.'

'You are threatening us,' Maurice said.

'Well, have it your own way. What's in a word? Situation's the same, whichever way you look at it. So what d'you say, boys? Do you take the money or don't you?'

There was a faint sound in the lobby. Barney Baker heard it, but he was not sure that any of the others did. It could have been the outer door softly opening and shutting.

He said: 'Stuff the money and stuff you, Jesse. We didn't come here to do a deal. We came to take revenge.'

'Revenge, is it?' Rackerman spoke mockingly. 'Oh dear! Was that what the shooters was for? Not much use to you over there, are they?' He pointed towards the guns on the mantelpiece. 'Fact is, boys, you ain't up to it. You're out of your depth. Still a bit wet behind the lugs, I'd say.'

He might have said more, but there was an interruption. The door was kicked open and Buster Jakes walked in. He was holding an Uzi submachine-gun in his hands.

Chapter Thirteen
LAST ACT

The Baker Boys stood up quickly and moved aside to give him a clear view of the other four. Tommy made a move to get at his pistol, but Jakes said one word:

'No!'

Tommy saw the muzzle of the Uzi pointing at him and decided not to be a dead hero. He stopped the move and kept his hands in view.

'Now,' Barney said, 'don't any of you lot make a move, because Buster is pretty good with that little gun, and we don't want any blood on the floor, do we?'

Rackerman was looking furious; the two heavies looked bewildered by this sudden turn of events; and Swan looked plain scared. At a word from his brother, Maurice moved round to the other side of the table and took the guns from the mantelpiece. He passed the revolver across to Barney and pocketed his own pistol. Then he relieved Tommy of the big automatic. He frisked Dod and found a flick-knife but no gun. Swan was clean, but Rackerman had a small Beretta tucked away. Maurice took this also.

Barney grinned at Rackerman, and there was a savagery in the grin that boded no good for the older man.

'Not up to it, I think you said, Jesse. Out of our depth, are we? A bit wet behind the lugs was the expression, wasn't it? Maybe you'd like to change your opinion now.'

Rackerman said nothing. He merely scowled.

Barney continued to taunt him. 'Thought we hadn't brought Buster along, didn't you? But we had. We just dropped him off before we got to the gate. He had his instructions – give us about ten minutes and then walk in with the gun.'

'Oh, very smart,' Rackerman sneered. 'But after all where does it get you?'

'Where does it get us? Why it gets us taking that revenge I was speaking about. Revenge for the killing of our dad.'

'You think I killed him? You must be off your trolley.'

'No, I'm not saying you killed him yourself. You're far too crafty for that. And besides, I don't believe you'd have the guts. But what I am saying is, you had him killed.'

'You can't prove that,' Rackerman said. 'Nobody can.'

'Why, Jesse,' Barney said mockingly, 'what makes you think I want to prove it? That's for the coppers. And I don't think they can do it either. But me and Maurie, we don't need any proof; we just know. So now I'm going to ask you a question, Jess. Who was the hit-man? Because we mean to deal with him too. All in good time, all in good time. So give us his name, Jess, because we really are interested, and it might be all the better for you to come clean, you know.'

'Go to hell,' Rackerman said.

'So you're going to be stubborn. Well, it's about what we'd've expected from a mule like you. But how about the rest of you?' He glanced at the others. 'Any of you feel like supplying the name, so's we can get this business tidied up and done with?'

None of them spoke, though Swan pulled nervously at his lower lip and looked decidedly unhappy. Barney made a mental note that he was a possible weak link.

Then Maurice said: 'I think we should be on the move. This can wait.'

Barney agreed. 'You could be right. No point in wasting more time here.' He turned to Jakes. 'You got the tape?'

'Sure,' Jakes said.

He reached into a pocket and brought out a roll of two-inch-wide green sticky tape. Barney took the tape, and he and his brother set about trussing the other men. They started on Rackerman, who did not submit without a struggle. In fact, he made himself such a nuisance that Maurice had to give him a few hefty slaps on the face to persuade him to co-operate. This did the trick, and in a minute or so Rackerman's arms were bound tightly to his sides with half a dozen turns of the sticky tape round his chest and waist. Another strip of the same material covered his mouth and effectively gagged him.

The remaining three, obviously having no desire to get the treatment from Maurice's heavy hand that the boss had suffered, made no resistance to the trussing and gagging, though Tommy and Dod uttered a string of obscenities before their power of speech was taken from them.

'Now let's go,' Barney said.

But before leaving they wiped everything they had touched in order not to leave any fingerprints. They took the briefcase containing the twenty-five thousand pounds, because, as Maurice remarked, it seemed a pity to let it be wasted.

Barney was the last to leave, wiping the doorknobs after him. He brought with him the keys to one of the vans standing in the yard, having persuaded Harry Swan to tell him where they were and which of the vans was in the best running order before sealing his lips. Swan had been very obliging in spite of receiving some black looks from Rackerman. There could be no doubt that the little man was hoping for lenient treatment from the brothers if he co-operated.

It was a clear cool night, with hardly a breath of wind and only the faint sound of traffic in the distance and a barking dog to be heard.

The van was in fact the blue Transit next to which the BMW was parked, and there was plenty of petrol in the tank. The trussed and bound men were helped into the back and made to sit or lie down on the floor. Maurice was to do the driving, with Jakes to accompany him. Barney would follow in the car.

They drove south, and out beyond the limits of Greater London they got themselves on to some minor roads in the more thinly populated parts of Surrey. Finally they came to the spot they had been heading for: a deserted gravel pit which the Baker Boys had discovered a few days earlier when they had been on a reconnaissance drive.

There was a rough track sloping down into the pit, and as they drove down it the headlights picked out some digging and grading machinery and a wooden hut on one side, looking rather dilapidated. Maurice stopped the Transit van close up to the opposite side of the pit which was like a cliff towering above it. Barney parked the BMW some distance away, switched off the engine and lights, got out and walked across to the van with a can of petrol he had taken from the boot of the car. He was also carrying a torch.

Maurice and Jakes had stepped out of the cab of the van, and now Maurice opened the rear doors. Barney handed the can of petrol to his brother and shone the torch in on the captives.

He said: 'You lot may be wondering why we've brought you all this way. Well, I'll tell you. This is where you get your punishment for arranging the murder of my father. This is a pretty deserted spot at this time of night, so even if you was to yell your heads off when we remove the gags nobody would hear you except us.' He turned to Jakes. 'Right, Buster, get them off.'

Jakes climbed into the van and ripped the sticky tape from the men's mouths. An operation painful enough to make Swan cry out. The other three were more stoical and made no sound.

'Now,' Barney said, 'who's going to tell us the name of the hit-man what blew my father's brains out?'

Nobody said anything, though Swan made a kind of whimpering sound and was shaking with fear.

'So maybe you've all forgotten,' Barney said. 'And maybe I'd better give your memories a jog by telling you what's going to happen to you if you don't cough up the info.' He turned to his brother. 'Right, Maurie. Just give 'em a taste of the juice.'

Maurice unscrewed the cap of the petrol can and splashed some of the liquid on to the captives. The reek of the spirit was strong in the van.

'We're going to burn you,' Barney said. 'That's if you don't tell us what we want to know.'

Suddenly Rackerman shouted: 'Damn you! You're going to do it anyway. What do we gain by telling you? That's what you brought us here for, so why fool around?'

Swan started to plead. 'Oh no! Please no! You can't do it; you can't.'

'Oh, we can, you know,' Barney said. 'Easy as falling off a log. But of course if one of you was to tell us what we want to know we could maybe spare him.'

'Don't any of you let him fool you,' Rackerman cried. 'He's just having you on. He would never let any of us go because that'd be leaving a witness to tell the tale.'

'Oh, I don't know,' Barney said; and he was looking hard at Swan. 'Maybe if the one we spared was to give his solemn word not to split on us we'd trust him. And maybe there is one of you we could trust. Just the one. It'd be a chance for him. And what would he have to lose when all's said and done?'

Swan licked his lips and said hoarsely: 'I'd promise.'

Barney smiled at him. 'And I think I could trust you. Not the others, of course. But you're different. You don't really fit in with them. Yes, I'd trust you.'

Rackerman was sitting beside Swan, their backs resting against the side of the van. He kicked the smaller man viciously on the leg.

'You fool! You can't believe him. He'd say anything to get you to talk.'

Swan gave a yelp when the kick landed, but this was all the notice he took of Rackerman. He spoke to Barney.

'I can't tell you the man's name. None of us can. We never knew it. Everything was arranged by a go-between.'

Barney could believe that. It was the way a bastard like Jesse Rackerman would go to work, keeping himself at a safe distance from the killer. But it made him no less of a murderer, no less a candidate for the brothers' vengeance. The others were merely tools, but they had gone along with it, raising no objection. He had to remember that; it made them guilty too.

'But you know who the go-between was?'

'Yes,' Swan said. 'If I tell you that, will you let me go?'

'You have my word,' Barney said.

'The man's name is Gage. Ambrose Gage.'

'Ah!' Barney said.

He had heard of Gage, but had never met the man. There had been a whisper, a name passed along the grapevine. If you wanted a certain type of job done he was the one to go to. So Gage had arranged the killing of Alfred Baker. That made him culpable too. Write down Ambrose Gage on the list. He had it coming to him.

'You'll find him in the Yellow Pages,' Swan said. 'He's got a warehouse down Plaistow way. Pukka business.'

'But he doesn't live there?'

'No. I think his house is in Chingford. Maybe that's in the Phone Book. I don't know. I've never been there.'

'Any family?'

'Not that I heard of. He's not married. Could be he lives alone.'

'Well thank you for the information, Harry,' Barney said. 'There's nothing else we ought to know?'

'Nothing I can think of.'

'Then we'll be saying goodbye. Don't look like we'll ever meet again.'

Swan was becoming alarmed. 'But you're going to let me go, aren't you?'

'Sorry. That won't be possible.'

'But you promised. You said if I told you what you wanted to know you'd set me free.'

'It just goes to show, doesn't it,' Barney said, 'that you shouldn't believe all you hear.'

Rackerman turned on Swan. 'You fool! You bloody fool! I warned you. Now he's got all he wanted and we've got nothing. Nothing at all.'

There was a curious sound coming from one of the heavies. It was Dod. He was crying.

Without waiting for orders Jakes now climbed into the van and began to bind the legs of the captives with more of the sticky tape. It was a way of ensuring that none of them escaped the final showdown. When he had finished Maurice poured more of the petrol on the men and the interior of the van. Meanwhile Barney had fetched a length of old cord from the car. He tied one end of it to Rackerman's left ankle and stretched the rest of it out to a distance of twenty yards or so from the van, while Maurice dribbled the remains of the petrol on to it.

The two of them and Jakes then stood at the end of the line and could hear voices coming from the van. These mingled in a strange mixture of pleading and cursing.

'Now,' Barney said, 'I reckon this is where the curtain goes up on the last act of tonight's show.'

He took a box of matches from his pocket, struck one and let it fall on the petrol-soaked cord. It ignited at once and the flame ran along the ground like something that was alive and eager to reach its journey's end. It got there in moments and there was a roar as the whole van took fire.

For a little while they could hear the screaming. But it did not last long. After that there was silence except for the hungry sound of the fire gutting the van.

'Time to go,' Barney said. 'You drive, Maurie.'

But there was one more job to be done before leaving. Jakes took a stiff broom from the boot of the car and proceeded to obliterate the footprints they had left in the gravel. Then the car was driven up the track to the road while he followed, walking backwards and brushing out his own footmarks and the traces of the tyre marks as he went. The car was waiting for him when he reached the hard road. He put the broom back in the boot and got in.

The flames from the burning Transit van were still visible as Maurice drove the car away.

Chapter Fourteen

ALIBI

Keele read about it in the paper. Some workers going to the gravel-pit in the morning had found the burnt-out van and what was left of the four bodies inside it. The van had been identified as one owned by a small haulage firm which traded under the name of Rackerman's Transport. Mr Rackerman was missing and it was feared that one of the dead bodies might have been his, though positive identification had not yet been made. Not surprisingly, the police were treating the case as murder.

Rona also read the report. She thought it was horrible.

'Do you think those people were burnt alive?'

'It doesn't say. It might not be easy to tell.'

'But somebody must know. The ones who drove the van and set fire to it. Do you think they'll be found?'

'Your guess is as good as mine.'

'But the police will be looking for them, won't they?'

'Of course they will. They always look for murderers. They don't always find them, though.'

Keele was not particularly interested in the incident. He was not familiar with the name of Rackerman and he had no reason to connect this case with the murder of Alfred Baker. As far as he could tell there was no evidence pointing to a link between the two, and therefore no way in which the four incinerated bodies could be any concern of his.

Later that day he was to alter his opinion on that point. Rona had gone to work and he was alone in the house when the telephone rang. He was surprised when he answered it to find that it was Ambrose Gage on the line. He had not expected to have any more contact with the man and he was none too pleased to hear his voice now.

'What the devil do you want?'

'Have you read the papers?' Gage asked.

Keele detected a note of concern in his voice. He sounded nervous; maybe even scared.

'Yes, I have.'

'The burnt-out van with the dead bodies. You read about that?'

'Yes.'

'Anything strike you about it?'

'Nothing in particular. Why?'

'Name Rackerman mean anything to you?'

'No. Why should it?'

'Because,' Gage said, 'he was the client. That last job. Rival gang. Wanted Baker out of the way. Thought I'd better tell you. Put you in the picture.'

He rang off, leaving Keele to digest this information at his leisure.

It was certainly not very pleasant information. It was probably not meant to be. Gage had sounded not at all happy. Keele guessed that he was quite certain that one of the dead men in the van was Rackerman, and that the others were associates of his. This had frightened Gage, that was for sure; and he had felt an urge to share his unease with Keele.

He saw clearly what Gage had been hinting at: that the murder of Rackerman had been a revenge killing. Carried out by whom? Why, the Baker Boys, of course. Keele knew about them, knew the reputation they had; though he had never had any contact with them. But how would they have known that Rackerman had engineered the killing of their father? Well, perhaps they had good reason to suspect him, and suspicion had been enough in their book.

Still, there was no need for Gage to feel threatened. They knew nothing of his involvement, did they? Unless perhaps they had extracted this information from Rackerman before killing him. That was certainly a possibility. And in that case Gage would be perfectly justified in feeling uneasy because of the part he had played in the affair.

And if Gage was next in line for the treatment, how did he, Martin Keele, stand? For it was he who had fired the fatal bullet and they would surely not ignore him.

But it would not come to that; they knew nothing of him.

Unless Gage told them.

But no; he would not do that, would he?

Well, on second thoughts, yes he would. Like a shot. Under pressure Gage would be no stoic. And he might feel that he owed Keele nothing now. In fact, he might give the information without any pressure at all, from sheer spite directed at his former associate.

So perhaps the threat should be removed in the one certain way it could be. He would have to think about that. And he had better not take too long over the thinking either. Because time might be fast running out.

Detective Inspector Morton had no doubt in his own mind regarding who it was who had burned the four men in the Transit van when the bodies had been identified. He knew quite a lot about the rivalry between the Rackerman lot and the Bakers, and he was not incapable of putting two and two together and coming up with four. The Baker Boys had of course been holding things back from him when he interviewed them. He had guessed at the time that they had a pretty shrewd idea of who had killed their father; and they were the sort who would not think twice about taking the law into their own hands.

So for him they were the prime suspects in this new case.

Detective Superintendent Milburn was inclined to agree. The particularly vicious nature of the killing gave it all the marks of a gangland feud.

'But have we anything to go on? Except suspicion.'

Morton had to admit that so far they had not. He had talked to the wives of Jesse Rackerman and Harold Swan, and each had given more or less the same story. On the fatal night their husbands had said they would be late at the office. Apparently they had arranged to have a business conference with some other men whose names they had not confided to their wives. This was not unusual and they had thought nothing of it. Neither woman had felt obliged to wait up for her husband, and neither of them had realised that she had had no sleeping partner until she had awakened in the morning.

Both women were upset, but not as upset as might have been expected of two wives suddenly bereaved in such a sickeningly brutal manner. Morton had a feeling that the husbands would not be greatly missed; and the expectation of handsome legacies to squander as they wished might seem ample compensation for the loss they had sustained.

The heavies who had died with Rackerman and Swan had not been married, and no one seemed likely to be devastated by their shuffling off the mortal coil. There would be next-of-kin to be informed, but that was not Morton's concern.

He had another talk with the Baker Boys and discovered, not altogether to his surprise, that they had alibis for the night in question. From early evening until late the next morning they had been at Barney's house in East Finchley, along with Buster Jakes and three women. From what they said Morton gathered that it had been some kind of orgy. There was nothing illegal about that on private premises, was there? Maurice inquired with an air of utter innocence.

Barney supplied the names and addresses of the women, which by some fortunate chance he had already written down, and said he was sure they would all corroborate what he had told the inspector.

'We had quite a time of it, one way and another, didn't we, Maurie?'

'We did that,' Maurice agreed. 'Next time maybe we'll invite you to come along and join in the fun, Inspector. You'd enjoy it. Take you out of yourself, it would.'

'Thank you,' Morton replied, somewhat acidly, 'but I have no desire to be taken out of myself.'

Nor did he get any pleasure in having the mickey taken by these two villains. They were laughing up their sleeves at him, taunting him with his inability to nail them. But one fine day he would catch them, and then maybe they would laugh on the other side of the face. Unfortunately, that day was not yet there, and for the present he had to endure their mockery and not give them the satisfaction of seeing him react to it with anger. Self-control, that was the ticket. His day would come.

He checked up on the women, knowing that it would be a fruitless exercise. All of them corroborated Barney Baker's story. They swore it was the truth, and would have done so on the Bible if they had owned such a thing. They were the sort who would have sworn to anything if they had been paid sufficiently well to do so. He attempted to catch them out by asking them to give some details regarding the house where the orgy was supposed to have taken place; but they were up to this ploy. It was evident that they knew it well, so it looked as though they had been there on other occasions, if not on this particular one.

He confided his frustration to the superintendent, who seemed able to accept the situation more phlegmatically.

'Ah, they're a smart pair of gallows-birds, those Baker Boys. They know their way around; that you can't deny.'

Morton did not deny it. But he thought the superintendent sounded half admiring of the two. Which to his way of thinking was morally wrong, because there was nothing admirable in being a clever criminal, damned if there was.

'One of these days they'll make a slip. They're cocking a snook at us now, but the luck won't always be with them. Eventually they'll come a cropper, and I just hope I'll be there to see it.'

'I hope so too,' Milburn said. 'But meanwhile of course we still have the murder of Alfred Baker on our hands. Do you think the killer could have been one of those burned in that van?'

'I doubt it. If we were right in thinking that was a contract job, our man wouldn't have been with that lot. That was the Rackerman gang. Good riddance to them, of course; but we still have to keep looking for the other guy.'

'And maybe the Baker Boys are looking too.'

'That wouldn't surprise me in the very least,' Morton said.

Chapter Fifteen

RUMPUS

It was an unfortunate confrontation that took place at Reagan's Bar in the West End. Keele and Rona had gone there after an evening at the theatre, not with any prior intention of doing so but because quite by chance they found themselves passing the entrance. Keele stopped walking, glanced up at the gaudy neon sign over the doorway and said:

'Shall we?'

Rona saw the lifted eyebrow and the faint smile, and guessed what he was suggesting. It would be a small celebration. It was here that they had first met, so short a time ago measured in days, and yet seemingly so long, since it was now as if they had known each other for all their lives.

'Why not?'

So small a decision, but one that was to have unforeseen and most unwelcome consequences for both.

'Come along then,' he said. And he took her arm and guided her inside.

The place was fairly crowded, and the atmosphere was hot and smoky and redolent of the mingling of a multitude of different odours. There were drinkers leaning on the bar and there were others standing around or sitting at the tables. Everyone seemed to be talking at once, and the hum of conversation rose like an ascending wave of sound to break upon the ornate ceiling overhead.

Keele forced his way to the bar and managed to catch the attention of a barman. When he had obtained the drinks, a gin-and-tonic for Rona and beer for himself, he found that she had claimed one of the small round tables that had just been vacated by another couple.

'Tell me,' she said, 'is this a place you came to regularly before that evening?'

He needed no telling what evening she was referring to; she could have meant only one.

'No,' he said. 'As a matter of fact I'd never been here before. And you?'

'Oh, a few times. Yes, quite a few times in fact.'

He thought of asking her whether she had been alone on those occasions, as she had been when he had encountered her for the first time. But he thought better of it. He was not sure he really wanted to know.

They had been there no more than ten minutes when the man appeared. He must have been in the place when they came in, but they had not seen him in the crowd. If he had been at the far end of the bar he would have been out of their sight. But now suddenly he was standing by the table and staring at them; and it was quite apparent that he was not quite sober. He was a rather plump-faced man, not bad-looking but not young; about forty perhaps.

'Well, well, well!' he said. 'If it isn't dearest Rona!'

'What do you want, Paul?' she said.

Keele could see that she was not well pleased to see the man, and he was not exactly delighted by the encounter himself.

The man said: 'Now that doesn't sound a very friendly way to greet an old acquaintance. And such an acquaintance

116

too. Don't I get to be introduced to your partner?'

She hesitated a moment and then said curtly: 'Martin, this is Paul.'

Keele nodded but said nothing.

'Paul Nickson actually,' the man said. 'She didn't tell you about me?'

Keele remained silent.

Nickson gave a laugh. 'No, I can see she didn't. Wouldn't want you to know maybe. Well, I can understand that. All have our little secrets, don't we?'

'Look, Paul,' Rona said, 'why don't you go away? Can't you see you're not wanted here?'

Nickson gave a drunken laugh. 'Now that's not nice. Not friendly at all. Time was when I'd have been made welcome.' He turned to Keele. 'I used to live with her, you know. You living with her now, old boy?'

Holding his anger under control with difficulty, Keele said: 'You heard her. She doesn't want you here. And I don't want you here either. So shove off.'

Nickson was not completely steady on his feet, but he stood his ground with the obstinacy of a drinker who has had just a little too much. 'And suppose I don't want to shove off? Suppose I mean to stay right here. I can if I like, you know.'

'Don't push your luck. You might come to regret it.' Keele was keeping his voice low but there was a warning in it. He was coldly angry with this interloper, and in a more suitable place would have dealt with him very severely. 'Don't push it, pal.'

Nickson ignored the warning. 'Name's Paul, not Pal. And I'll push my luck as far as I damn well please. So what are you going to do about it?'

Keele was near enough to put a hand on his arm and push him away. Nickson reeled a little, regained his balance and

117

took a swing at Keele's jaw. The blow missed its mark because Keele leaned back and let it pass. He gave Nickson a shove in the chest and the man fell over backwards.

At this instant Keele was aware of a flash of light and a clicking sound, and he caught sight of a man with a camera only a few feet away. The altercation had attracted the interest of other people, who were staring at the three persons involved. It was all the kind of thing he would most have wished to avoid, because no good would come of it, and maybe a lot of bad.

He heard Rona's voice in his ear, and she was speaking with considerable urgency. 'For goodness' sake come away, Martin. Let's go; let's go.'

She was tugging at his sleeve and he knew that the wisest course would be to do what she was advising – to get to hell out of there before a bad situation turned to worse. It was just damned rotten luck that there should have been a photographer on hand to take a snapshot of what was happening at the crucial moment, but there was nothing he could do about that; the damage had been done.

Nickson was struggling to get to his feet and looking pretty damned angry and ready to cause more trouble. There was no sense in waiting for him to do that, so he hesitated no longer but made for the exit with Rona still clinging to his arm.

Nobody tried to stop them, and a moment later they were on the pavement in the cool night air and walking briskly away from Reagan's Bar, which he heartily wished they had never entered.

They spoke very little on the way back to his house. And when they were inside he still asked no questions, though there were enough of them waiting to be asked and on the tip of his tongue.

Finally it was she who broke the ice.

'You want to know all about him, don't you?'

Keele said nothing, just waited for her to go on. Which she did, after a brief hesitation.

'Well, it's true what he said of course. We were living together until I threw him out.'

'Why did you do that?'

'Because he became insufferable.'

'I can understand that,' Keele said. Two minutes of Nickson's company had been enough for him. 'When did this happen?'

Again she hesitated, but then said: 'The day I met you.'

'Oh, as recently as that! So I caught you on the rebound. Is that it?'

'No, that isn't it. It wasn't like that at all. You've got to believe me, it wasn't. What had gone before made no difference, no difference whatever. You and me, well that was something that would have had to happen whenever and wherever we'd met. At least as far as I was concerned. I thought it was the same for you. But maybe I was wrong about that.'

'You should have told me,' he said.

'About Paul? Perhaps I would have, eventually. But was it the kind of thing to blurt out when we were just getting to know each other? And besides, what have you told me about yourself?'

He could not deny that she had a point there. Neither of them had felt it necessary to reveal any of their past to the other. The present had been all that counted.

She was looking at him anxiously. 'What happened tonight isn't going to make any difference, is it? To us, I mean.'

He thought it might make a difference, but not in the way she meant. That damned photographer had snapped a

119

picture of him hitting Nickson; and that could be bad. He always avoided being photographed if he could manage it; but this time he had been taken by surprise. There might be no evil consequences, but who could tell? He just wished it had not happened. Damn that bastard, Nickson!

Rona was still gazing at him, as though trying to read his mind. He reached out in a gesture of reconciliation and took her hand.

'Forget it,' he said. 'Let's go to bed.'

The picture appeared in the next morning's later editions of the *Comet*. Apparently the photographer in Reagan's Bar was one of their staff, and he had got the snapshot to the paper without delay when he had found out from one of the barmen the identity of the woman concerned. It transpired that this man had talked to her on quite a few occasions when she had been there by herself.

It was not on the front page, but was included in one of the gossip columns with the caption: 'Rag-Bag Rona in Rumpus at Reagan's'. Then there was a paragraph which read: 'Rona Wickham, co-owner of chic Chelsea boutique, the Rag-Bag, was last evening involved in a scuffle at Reagan's Bar in the West End. It appears that Miss Wickham was having a quiet guzzle with her boyfriend when they were accosted by another man. A brief contretemps led to fisticuffs, and the second man was left lying on the floor while Miss W and the boyfriend beat a hasty retreat from the scene. Neither of the gentlemen involved has been identified. Anyone seeking further enlightenment should perhaps pay a visit to the Rag-Bag, which we are informed is much esteemed by the cognoscenti.'

Keele did not take the *Comet*, and it was not until Miss Wickham arrived at the Rag-Bag to start work that she learned that she had got herself into the news. One of the assistants had picked up a copy of the paper on her way to the boutique and had spotted the picture and read the piece. On arrival she had shown it to Miss Somers; who had laughed.

Kimberley, the assistant in question, laughed too when she saw that it was safe to do so. 'It is rather funny, isn't it?'

'Yes, but don't tell Rona so. She might not be quite so amused by it.'

'Do you know who the men are?'

'Yes. But I'm not telling you or anyone else.'

The girl seemed disappointed. 'I thought one of them looked rather like the man who was here with her the other day.'

'Possibly he does. But if you want to know who he is you'll have to ask her.'

Kimberley said she would not dare; and Miss Somers said she would probably be well advised not to, unless she wanted to have her head bitten off.

'Oh, my God!' Rona said when she had seen the picture and read the item. 'This is just what we did not want. Martin will be furious.'

'I don't see why he should be,' Jean said. 'It's pretty innocuous. It may do us a bit of good though. It's publicity for the boutique.'

'Not the sort I would wish for. I suppose there'll be a lot of cranks doing what this so-called newspaper advises them to do. You won't tell them anything, will you?'

'Not if you don't want me to.'

'I don't. And now I think I'd better give Martin a call and warn him about this.'

He was still at home when she rang; and as she had expected he was not at all pleased.

'Damn that photographer. He ought to be shot. It's an invasion of privacy. There should be a law against it.'

She thought he was making rather too much of a fuss about it, and she did her best to mollify him.

'But there's no real harm done, is there? In a couple of days it'll simply be forgotten.'

'Maybe so. And maybe not so.'

'Well, even if it isn't, what does it really matter? It's not the end of the world.'

He did not answer that. She heard him slam the telephone down, and she knew he was in a rage. She wondered why. It seemed such a trifling matter to be so concerned about.

Chapter Sixteen

A CALL ON GAGE

After he had received the telephone call Keele went out and bought a copy of the *Comet*. It was the kind of paper he never looked at as a rule: one of the raucous gutter tabloids; a paper for semi-literates and dimwits, which pandered to the xenophobic prejudices of the masses and the lecherous tastes of the male reader.

He turned at once to the page where the photograph taken at Reagan's Bar was reproduced. The alliterative caption was typical of the paper's literary style and set his teeth on edge. He glanced through the report with increasing annoyance, and then took a closer look at the photograph. It was not, he thought, a good picture of himself; and that was a point in its favour. But was it good enough? Would the people who had seen him on the night of Alfred Baker's murder recognise it as a photograph of him if they saw it? That was the question.

He felt he could rule out the drunk. He would not have been seeing too clearly, even if the light had been a good deal better. The two skinheads had not had a very good sight of him either, because the nearest streetlamp had been out of action, and where the car had stood there had been a lot of shadow. Of course if they read a paper at all, which was doubtful, the *Comet* would be the sort they would be likely to choose; but there were others in that field with bigger circulations, so there was a good chance that they would not see the picture or would take no notice of it if they did.

This left Miss Mandy Cant. Undoubtedly she had had a very clear sight of him indeed. The light in the bathroom had been good and she had been very close to him. So of all the witnesses she would be the one who presented the greatest threat. But perhaps she would never see the paper. And even if she saw it and recognised one of the men in the photograph as the one who had locked her in the bathroom at The Bakery, would she report this fact to the police? Certainly she had promised more than once, had promised with much vehemence, that she would never put the finger on him. But could he rely on that promise now that she was no longer in any immediate danger from him? He doubted it. People could be so ungrateful.

He dumped the paper and went to George's Gym for a work-out. George greeted him as he always did, with cordiality but not effusion.

'Nice to see you, Mr Keele. Not been around lately. Business taking up your time?'

'Yes, business,' Keele said.

He tried to detect anything odd in George's manner which might indicate that he had read the item in the *Comet* and had recognised one of the men in the photograph. A sidelong glance, a lift of the eyebrow perhaps. But there was nothing. He might have asked George if he read the *Comet*, but that would have been stupid; it would merely have aroused the man's curiosity.

There were few other clients in the gym. One or two of them nodded to him or made a remark on the weather, that subject of eternal interest to the Englishman, but nobody gave him a curious look or one of those fleeting smiles that might have indicated a knowledge of the affair at Reagan's Bar and the added knowledge that he had been one of the men involved.

He had lunch at the club, Rona having said that she would be unable to join him at midday because of pressure of work, and it was the same there. No smirks were to be detected on the faces of the employees with whom he came into contact, though he watched them closely. The members of course were more likely to read the *Daily Telegraph* or the *Financial Times* than a rag like the *Comet*, but the whisper might have got around. However, apparently it had not, and he felt reassured.

Not that there would have been any threat to him even if all these people had discovered that he had had a set-to with another man in a West End bar. It would have been slightly embarrassing but nothing more; an incident that would have been quickly forgotten. No, the only possible danger would come from the four witnesses who had encountered him at or near the scene of a certain crime. And of these only Miss Cant presented a serious menace.

He had of course had it in his power to eliminate that danger and he had not done so. Had he been too soft? Perhaps so. And was it still not too late to remove the danger? Possibly not. And yet he knew that he would not do it. He had passed up the chance when it had been offered, and that was how the situation would remain. Do what she might, Miss Cant was safe from him.

There remained, however, Ambrose Gage, who could be the key to a threat from a different quarter: not the police but the Baker Boys.

Ought he not to do something about that?

He left it for a couple more days before deciding that he

ought. His fear was that he might already have left it too late.

Rona was surprised when he told her that he had an appointment and would be going out.

'At this hour?'

It was ten o'clock in the evening.

'Yes, at this hour.'

'So who is this appointment with?'

'A man. You don't know him.'

'At least you could tell me his name.'

'It's not important.'

If he told her the name and she read later about the discovery of the dead body of a man with that same name it might give her ideas he would not have wished her to have.

But she was persistent. 'Why the secrecy? What harm would it do if you were to tell me?'

He saw that it would only increase her curiosity if he still refused. So he said: 'Very well. His name is Stephen Wooldridge and he lives in Bushey. He wants my advice on a piece of business he's contemplating.'

'How very odd,' she said. And he could tell that she was sceptical of this story. 'And so very late too.'

'Look,' he said, 'I know what you're thinking. That it's a woman.'

'And it isn't?' She gave a lift of the eyebrows.

'My dear Rona,' he said, 'why on earth would I want another woman when I have you?' And he kissed her.

This argument seemed to convince her that he was telling the truth, and she just said:

'When are you likely to be back?'

'Well, it's quite a way. Could be after midnight. But there's no need for you to wait up.'

'Then I won't.'

He drove out to Chingford in the Jaguar, taking the revolver with him. He had managed to remove it from the safe without being observed by Rona, and it was loaded and had the silencer fitted.

Chingford was out towards Epping Forest, and there were some trees in the neighbourhood of Gage's house, which was an old building standing in a fairly large but neglected garden. There was a gate standing open and a weedy drive curving round to the front door. Keele knew that Gage lived alone in this rambling old structure that was far too big for him but which had come to him as a legacy many years ago. There was a woman who came in two days a week to make a stab at keeping the place clean and tidy, but she was fighting a losing battle against the dirt and was probably resigned to it. She did Gage's washing as well.

When he parked the Jaguar by the front door Keele could see no light showing in any of the windows, and he wondered whether Ambrose had gone to bed. It was quite possible, but it would make no difference. Alfred Baker had been in bed and it had not saved him.

He went to the front door under the brick porch and hauled on the old-fashioned bell-pull. It made a harsh grating sound and set a bell ringing somewhere inside the house. The enveloping darkness and that oddly distant ringing gave him the impression of a place that had been completely deserted, an empty shell. Could Ambrose Gage have gone away? When he had rung through with that brief piece of information regarding Rackerman he had certainly sounded unhappy, frightened even, as though fearful of what the next move of the Baker Boys might be after they had dealt so savagely with the rival gang.

Perhaps, therefore, he had been so fearful that he had felt he could only save himself from a similar fate by instant flight. But where would he have gone? And what about his business? Would he abandon everything in a moment under this goading of terror? It was possible. And yet it seemed improbable. The man was more likely to have gone to bed, and either he had not been wakened by the ringing of the bell or was determined not to pay any attention to it.

Keele decided to try the door. He was wearing his black leather gloves, and now he turned the knob and discovered to his surprise that the door was not locked. It opened under the pressure of his hand with a slight creaking sound. This seemed to indicate tht Gage had not gone away, since he would hardly have left the house open to anyone who might have felt inclined to walk in. So it looked as though he had gone to bed without locking up. It must have been an oversight, but it made things simpler for Keele.

The entrance hall was in complete darkness and there was no sign of any light elsewhere in the house. Keele preferred not to hunt around for switches and fetched a torch from the car to show him the way around. When he returned with this he closed the door behind him and began his search for Gage. The house had a characteristic odour about it that was not at all pleasant, and he guessed that it would not have been difficult to find evidence of dry-rot in much of the woodwork. There could have been wet-rot and mildew as well.

The obvious place to look for Gage was in his bedroom, and Keele made his way to the wide stairs which rose from the hall to the first floor landing. Some of the steps creaked loudly under his weight, but he disregarded this. If the sound were to awaken Gage it would make no difference.

The landing gave access to a number of doors, and he began opening them one by one, searching for Gage's bedroom. There was only one that appeared to have been in recent use, and Gage was not in it. The bed was made but it was unoccupied.

Keele was puzzled. Could Ambrose have fallen asleep in

an armchair in one of the downstairs rooms? This seemed improbable, since in that case the light would have been left on. So had he been abducted? That was certainly a possibility; but before accepting it as a fact it would be advisable to carry out a search of the ground floor.

He retreated down the stairs and began looking into the various rooms. He found no one in any of them. He tried the kitchen last. It was big and had never been totally modernised. There was still an old porcelain sink with brass taps, one of which was steadily dripping into it. There was a gas cooker of antique design, and a tall wooden dresser stood against one wall. In the middle of the room was a plain deal table, scrubbed into ridges in the course of many years of use. There was no sign of Ambrose Gage.

The beam of the torch revealed a door at the far end of the kitchen; it looked as though it might possibly open on to a cupboard. It seemed highly improbable that the man would be in there, but Keele decided to take a look nevertheless. When he opened the door he discovered that there was not a cupboard behind it but one of those large old-time pantries or larders with whitewashed walls and a lot of shelves and a meat-safe.

The ceiling was high and there was a rough oak beam in the middle of it. In this was a row of stout iron hooks, from which smoked hams might once have hung. There were no hams hanging from any of them now, but suspended from one was an even heavier burden. It was Ambrose Gage.

There was a rope round Gage's neck and the rope was attached to the hook. Gage's feet were six inches from the tiled floor, and he was quite motionless, his head turned slightly to one side, face tinged purple, eyes bulging, mouth twisted in a fixed grimace; all of which gave him a most repellent appearance.

There was a wooden stool lying overturned not far from

his dangling feet. He had perhaps been standing on it just before his death. And then perhaps he had kicked it away as suicides did when they wished to hang themselves.

But why would Gage have wished to kill himself? Because of his fear of the Baker Boys? To take his own life was a certain way of escaping from their attentions, but it was a pretty drastic one, to say the least. So had Gage had other reasons for committing suicide? Business worries? Failing health perhaps? A feeling that life had nothing more to offer and he would be better off in some other world?

Keele did not accept any of these. In fact he did not believe the suicide theory at all. He would have made a bet that this was a case of murder made to look like suicide. Moreover, he did not have much difficulty in guessing who had carried out the job.

The Baker Boys had beaten him to it.

Chapter Seventeen
CAT-AND-MOUSE

She woke when he climbed into bed with her.

She said: 'Oh, so you're back. What time is it?'

'It's a quarter to one,' he said.

'It took you long enough. Did the business go well?'

'No,' he said. 'Actually it did not.'

He might have told her that it had gone extremely badly; in the worst kind of way from his point of view. For he did not believe that the Baker Boys would have been content just to kill Gage; they would have wanted something from him first; and that something would have been the name of the hit-man who had put the bullet into their father's head. And they probably would not even have had to torture Gage to make him talk; threats would have been enough. They might even have promised to spare his life if he told them what they wanted to know. And he, in his bitterness with Keele for pulling the plug on their business relations, might have been only too willing to provide the name. And of course it had not saved him in the end, because those he was dealing with were not the kind to feel obliged to honour their word.

He could see how it was now. The Baker Boys were carrying out a systematic operation to avenge their father's death. First they had dealt with the instigators of the contract; now they had punished the arranger of the murder; and the next on the list, the final one that would complete the set, was none other than Martin Keele. He was the prime target and the only one left.

This, of course, was to take for granted that it had been the Baker Boys who had turned the Rackerman lot to cinders and had arranged Gage's death by hanging. And there was no proof. Rackerman and his associates might have been killed by another rival gang, and Gage might have hanged himself as it appeared. But Keele did not believe it; not for a moment did he even begin to believe it. He knew what he knew.

So he was now the target; the one they had been working their way to from the start. And he did not like it; did not like it at all.

It was not the first time he had been a target; but the previous occasions had been years ago and he had not been alone. He had had comrades in arms and that had made it all so very different. Suddenly he felt terribly exposed. He could not tell when they would strike or how they would do it. Now he would be forever looking over his shoulder; he would have to be forever on his guard. And he did not even know what the Baker Boys looked like; or the gorilla who would no doubt he hunting with them.

He said: 'It didn't go at all according to plan. Everything went wrong.'

'Oh,' she said, 'I'm so sorry about that. Is it bothering you very much?'

She was observant, he thought; she had sensed that he was worried and was maybe inviting him to share the worry with her. He would have liked to, but he could not. On this matter more than any other he was unable to confide in her, even though it affected her now as well as him, simply because they were so close, one to the other.

He said, as though changing the subject; although, if only she had known, there was a connection: 'I feel I could use a change of scene for a while. What would you say to a long honeymoon in the sun?'

'We're not married,' she said. 'Were you proposing we should have a wedding and then go?'

'No. Afterwards perhaps. There's no hurry for that.'

'But there is for the honeymoon?'

She sounded amused, but somewhat puzzled also.

'I thought it would appeal to you,' he said. 'Doesn't it?'

'Oh yes; it appeals to me greatly.'

'So?'

'When were you proposing to leave?'

'At once.'

'But that's not possible. There'd be so much to arrange.'

'Things can always be speeded up if you really put your mind to them.'

'Well, I don't know. How long were you thinking about being away?'

'A month, say.'

He was thinking that if he could leave the country for a time he could take stock of the situation, make plans. If no one was told where they were going there would be no way the Baker Boys could follow them.

'A month! Are you forgetting the Rag-Bag?'

'Surely Jean and the girls could look after the boutique.'

'It would be throwing rather a burden on her.' She sounded doubtful. 'I don't know that I could do that. It really would be asking rather a lot.'

'You could do the same for her later.'

'Well,' she said, 'I'll have to think about it.'

'Don't take too long. Give me an answer in the morning and I'll make the arrangements.'

'Have you thought of somewhere to go?'

'Yes, but I'm not telling you. I want it to be a surprise.'

'But I shall have to tell Jean.'

'There's no need. There's no need to tell anyone. It's none of their business where we go.'

'Well, if that's the way you want it.' She spoke doubtfully, still not entirely convinced that it was a good idea.

'It is.'

She was silent for a while, and he thought she had gone to sleep again. But then she said:

'There's something you're not telling me, isn't there?'

'Is that what you think?'

'Yes, it is. Has something happened? Something that makes it necessary for you to get away for a time?'

'What could have happened to do that?'

'I don't know. That's why I'm asking.'

He thought for a moment or two and came to the conclusion that perhaps it would be best to tell her part of the truth, if not all of it.

'All right then,' he said, 'I'll admit I do need to make a move. For a time at least.'

'Oh dear!' she said. 'Are you in trouble with the police?'

He gave a laugh. 'Oh no; it's nothing like that. I haven't committed any crime.' And that was a lie if ever there was one; but he had to tell it. 'Don't worry. It'll all come right in the end.'

'Which is as much as to say it's not all right just now?'

'Don't worry,' he said again. 'Just don't worry. Trust me.'

But he knew that he had said enough to ensure that she did worry. And since it was apparent to her that there was some pressing need for him to leave the country for a while, she agreed to tackle Jean in the morning about the month of absence from the business.

With that settled, he determined to get things started as soon as possible the next day. He saw no reason why they should not be on the move within a couple of days, and meanwhile he would carry the revolver around with him when he went out during the day. He would have kept it under his pillow at night, but he could hardly have done so without revealing it to Rona, and this would have been certain to alarm her. Above all he had to conceal from her the fact that his life was in danger and that this was the true reason why he had to leave the country without delay.

It was when he was returning to the house the following day after a visit to a travel agency that he saw the car parked by the kerb on the opposite side of the road. There were three men sitting in it. He had never seen any of them before, but he guessed at once that the two in the front were the Baker Boys and that the tough-looking one in the back was the late Alfred Baker's minder.

None of them was doing anything; they were just sitting there, waiting. And he knew what they were waiting for.

The crazy notion came into his head that he might walk up to the car and shoot all three of them where they sat. He had the revolver with him, and it would have been easy. But of course it was out of the question; he could never have got away with it. To carry out such a slaughter almost on his own doorstep would have been the height of folly.

Nevertheless, he did walk across the road, and he tapped on the window of the car on the passenger side. It was Barney Baker who lowered the window and looked at him.

'Yes?'

Keele said: 'Are you looking for somebody?'

'Do we look like we're looking for anybody?' Barney asked.

Keele made no answer to that. He just gave the men in the car a cold stare, shifting his gaze from one to another.

'Well,' Maurice said, 'I guess you'll certainly know us

when you see us again.'

'Shall I see you again?'

'Now that's the big question, innit? Me, I'd say it's likely. But you never know, do you?'

'No, you don't,' Keele said. 'Nothing's certain in this bad old world. Except death.'

'Ah!' Barney said, with a laugh. 'That's certain, right enough. But maybe you're the one to know a lot about that.'

'As much as the next man.'

'Or even more?'

'Yes,' Keele said. 'Maybe even more.'

He turned and walked away. And all the while he was crossing the road he was half expecting a bullet in the back; because they could have shot him there and driven away, and there was nobody around just at that moment to be a witness to what they had done. He felt a chill in the spine, and he cringed a little; but he refused to quicken his pace, and he reached the front door and no shot had come. So he let himself into the house and locked the door behind him and breathed more freely again.

But he knew that the danger had not gone away, and that it would continue to be present until he was out of the country.

In the car Maurice was saying: 'So now we know what the bastard looks like and he knows us. Now it's all out in the open. And I gotta say this for him: he's cool. He really is one cool customer, is our Mr Martin Keele.'

'Which was to be expected,' Barney said. 'You need to be cool in his line of business.'

'There's another thing we know too. That information Gage handed us before we topped him was kosher.'

'I never doubted it. He was too bloody scared to lie.'

'So what do we do now?' Jakes said. 'Do we go in an' finish the job?'

'Now, now, Buster,' Barney said, 'don't be so impatient. All in good time. Let him sweat it out for a bit. I meanter say, once he's dead that's the end of it – finito. No, we'll keep him hanging on for a few days, not knowing when we'll strike or where. Cat-and-mouse, Buster, cat-and-mouse. We're the cats and he's the mouse. Right?'

'Well, it's your say-so,' Jakes said.

But he sounded unconvinced. There was no doubt that he would have gone for the quick kill and no messing around. But he was not the boss.

The discovery of Gage's body was made by the woman who did the chores for him. It so happened that the day after the hanging was one of those when she came in. It was such a shock to her to see him hanging there from the meat-hook that she almost fainted on the spot. She said she came over all trembly like and had to sit down in the kitchen and collect herself.

When she had collected herself she got on the telephone to the police, and they were there very quickly to cut Gage down. It looked like suicide, and it was no front page news. Detective Inspector Morton heard about it, but he saw no connection between it and his investigation, so it was of no interest to him and he immediately forgot about it.

Ambrose Gage was carted off to the mortuary and an inquest was arranged for a later date.

Chapter Eighteen
A FAVOUR

'He wants you to go away with him for a month?' Miss Somers said. 'A whole month?'

'Yes. He calls it a honeymoon.'

'Without a wedding?'

'Yes.'

'Do you want to go?'

'Not if it'll be too much of a burden to you.'

'Ah, so now you're making it my decision. I don't know whether I can take that responsibility.'

'But can you manage without me? That's the question.'

'Of course I can. You didn't imagine you were indispensable, did you?'

Miss Somers gave a smile to indicate that this was just banter and not to be taken seriously.

'No, but—'

'Look, Rona, if you want to go away for a month, it's okay by me. But I do wonder whether you're doing the right thing.'

'Why wouldn't I be?'

'Well, it's not nearly as long as that since you first met Martin. How much do you really know about him even now? Has he for instance introduced you to any of his family?'

'No. They don't live in London. And besides, it seems there's not much love lost between him and them. He says he hasn't been to see any of them in ages, and doesn't intend to.'

'Um! Has he filled in any of the blanks in his life before he got himself hooked up with you?'

'Well, no,' Miss Wickham answered somewhat reluctantly. 'But there'll be plenty of time for that later.'

'On this honeymoon for instance?'

'Yes.'

'Where are you going?'

'I don't know. He wants it to be a surprise.'

'So how will I get in touch with you?'

'Do you need to? Martin doesn't want anyone to know. That way, he says, no one can bother us.'

This too seemed to raise doubts in Miss Somers's mind. 'It all sounds rather weird to me. But I suppose you know what you're doing.'

'Oh, you can be sure of that,' Miss Wickham said.

But the fact was that she was not entirely sure herself. There was something odd about the whole project: the suddenness, the haste, the secrecy regarding the destination. She trusted Martin of course; she had to trust the man she was so deeply in love with; but she could have wished that he had been more open about so many things. And after all, what did she know about him?

'Anyway,' she said, 'I'll send you a card from wherever it is.'

'Yes,' Miss Somers said, 'do that. And have a good time.'

Detective Superintendent Reginald Milburn and Detective Inspector Frank Morton were still trying without success to find the killer of Alfred Baker. They just could not get a solid lead, and it was very frustrating, as were all cases on which you spent a lot of time and energy and in the end got nothing in return for your trouble.

It was Morton's opinion that the murder of Rackerman and his lot still presented the most promising line of inquiry.

'There's no doubt in my mind, sir, that Jesse Rackerman was the instigator of the Baker killing. What happened to him was almost certainly in revenge.'

Milburn was not prepared to argue with him on this point. 'I think we can take that for granted, but where does it get us with the Baker Boys shoving their damned alibi up our noses? We can't get anything out of them.'

'I think maybe I should have another word with the women. Perhaps I could jog their memories in the matter of who Rackerman had arranged to meet that night.'

'I doubt whether much will come of it,' Milburn said, 'but go if you want to.'

Neither Mrs Rackerman nor Mrs Swan was at home when Morton called, but he traced them to the Wandsworth premises of Rackerman Transport. Apparently they were there for a conference with the firm's solicitor, a Mr Ahmed Shafferti, who appeared to be of Middle Eastern origin.

The conference, so Morton was informed, had to do with the winding up of the business, which could no longer be carried on now that Jesse Rackerman and his cousin had passed away in such an unfortunate manner. Mr Shafferti was just leaving; but before departing he assured the women that if they had any problems they had only to get in touch with him and he would be only too willing to assist them in any way he could.

'My door is always open and I am at your service.'

He made a little bow to the ladies, gave a curt nod to the inspector, and went to his car almost at a trot, as though his time were so valuable he could not bear to waste a moment of it.

141

'A very obliging man,' Morton observed drily. He knew a thing or two about Mr Shafferti and had heard him described as being as slippery as an eel. But in his opinion that description would have fitted a large section of the legal profession.

'He's a dear,' Mrs Rackerman said. She was a plump ash-blonde in her forties and had probably been quite a dazzler in her younger days. 'He did a lot of work for poor Jesse.'

Morton did not doubt it. He was the kind of lawyer Rackerman would have used.

Mrs Swan was red-haired and one of the thin and wiry kind, with teeth that were a shade too prominent for everyone's taste. She said:

'And what can we do for you, Inspector?'

'I thought,' Morton said, 'you might have remembered something that would help with the detection of your husbands' killers. Some little point that might have escaped you when I saw you last.'

They shook their heads.

'It's a mystery to us who would want to kill them,' Mrs Rackerman said.

'But you knew, I imagine, that they had enemies?'

'Ah, who doesn't?'

'I meant someone extra special. Someone who might bear a grudge against Mr Rackerman in particular. Maybe for something he had done. Perhaps to injure that person.'

He was giving them an opportunity to come up with the name of Baker. He was pointing them in the direction of the Baker Boys and inviting them to mention that pair of villains so that they could go on from there. But they were having none of it. Either they knew nothing of the feud or they were shy of mentioning it. Perhaps they feared reprisals from the Bakers.

There were piles of papers lying on the table in what had been the office. No doubt Ahmed Shafferti had been going through these with them. He guessed that this was where that other meeting had taken place, the one that had led to death by burning.

'I suppose,' he said, 'you've found nothing amongst these papers to indicate who Mr Rackerman and Mr Swan were conferring with that night when they failed to come home?'

'Nothing,' Mrs Rackerman said.

'But this is where the conference was to take place?'

'So Jesse said.'

Morton could imagine what had taken place. The Bakers, assisted by their man Jakes, had overpowered the other lot; perhaps by some trick. Then they had trussed them up and carried them away in one of Rackerman's own vans. But how had they managed to do that? Rackerman would have been wary of them; he had been no fool and there had been the two heavies with him. And yet he had let the Baker Boys win the game. He must have made some slip, some miscalculation, but it was pointless to try guessing what it might have been.

He had to come to the conclusion that there was nothing here that was going to help him. It had been a waste of time coming, because the two women, if they did know anything, were obviously determined not to tell it. He wondered just how much Shafferti would succeed in pulling out of the wreckage for them – with a useful percentage for himself, of course. And he guessed that this was what they were really interested in. Perhaps, if the truth were told, they were very glad that the Baker Boys had done this little job on their husbands. They were certainly shedding no tears over the matter. He had never seen a pair of mourners more dry-eyed.

That, Morton thought, was a measure of the regard that

some women had for their partners in life. He was a bachelor himself and tended to take a rather cynical view of the married state.

He reported his lack of success to Milburn when he got back.

'It was a wasted errand. I could get nothing out of the women.'

'Perhaps they know nothing.'

'Maybe that's so. But I know one thing – they're happy. It looks to me like the Baker Boys did them the biggest favour they ever had by knocking off their loving menfolk.'

'You think that's why they're saying nothing? They feel they owe it to the Boys?'

'I wouldn't go so far as that. They'll grab what's coming to them, but I don't think there'll be a lot of gratitude swilling around. Not from that pair. Hard as flint. They could be thinking of their own skins, though. Maybe the way they figure it, if they say nothing to turn the heat on the Baker Boys they'll be in no danger of reprisals from that quarter. If you've got any sense you don't fool around with people who wouldn't think twice about making a bonfire of you.'

'So we're still left without a lead.'

'That's so. I suppose we'll just have to stick around and hope that something turns up.'

As it happened, they had to stick around for a few more days before something did turn up. And when it did it had nothing whatever to do with the Rackerman lot.

Meanwhile, the Baker Boys were biding their time and leaving Keele to sweat it out. They sent Jakes in his car to sit outside the house in Kensal Green, and Keele saw him there and guessed what the game was.

He did not like it. It is never much fun being the mouse in

144

a game of cat-and-mouse; the fun is all for the cat. But there are times when the cat becomes over-confident and gives the mouse a bit too much rope. And then it's down the hole in a flash and the mouse is laughing.

So maybe the Baker Boys would give him too much rope.

Maybe they would be kicking themselves later.

Maybe.

Just maybe.

Time would tell.

Chapter Nineteen
THE NAME

Miss Amanda Cant did not see the report of the rumpus in Reagan's Bar until a few days after it appeared in the press. She did not read the *Comet*; in fact she read no newspaper regularly. She was not much interested in what went on in the world beyond that which she could observe with her own two eyes. And quite a lot of that was pretty dull stuff too in her opinion.

So it was not until a sheet of newsprint from the *Comet* drifted up to her feet as she was sitting on a bench and eating a sardine sandwich in Hyde Park that she was made aware of the incident at Reagan's involving two men and a woman.

She glanced down at the somewhat ragged and dirty piece of paper and the picture caught her eye. It made her sit up and take notice at once; for one of the men looked very much like the one she had last seen holding a gun in his hand in the bathroom of the late Alfred Baker's house, The Bakery.

She picked up the paper and examined the photograph more closely; and though she could not be absolutely certain, she felt that if this was not indeed the man who had shot Mr Baker, he was very much like him.

The report of the incident served neither to confirm nor discredit the impression, and she now found herself in a quandary. Ought she to go to the police and tell them she believed that this man, who was not named in the report, was the one who had locked her in the bathroom after shooting Mr Baker? Or would this simply mean more unwanted bother for her?

Miss Cant was a person who decided nearly all her actions on the principle of doing only what promised to be of most benefit to herself. She had grown up in a tough school where your first concern was for number one, and to hell with everybody else. So the fact that she had promised the man with the gun that she would never put the finger on him carried no weight with her now. Nor did she feel that she owed him anything for sparing her life, seeing that if it had not been for him that life would never have been in danger. Besides which, had the bastard not robbed her of the payment which should by rights have been coming to her?

Nevertheless, it was against her principles to approach the police voluntarily. They were her natural enemies, and the less she saw of them the better she liked it. So on the whole her inclination was to do nothing about the matter. Let the coppers work things out for themselves. They got paid for it, didn't they?

However, she did not completely rule out the possibility of taking action. She would think things over very carefully, giving due weight to all the pros and cons before coming to a final decision; and for the present she would keep the piece of newspaper to use or not to use as she thought fit.

She folded it carefully and put it in her handbag and finished eating her sardine sandwich.

Off and on she thought about the matter for a few more days, unable to make up her mind. And in the end it was the possibility of gaining some advantage for herself that influenced her decision. Her reasoning was that if she helped the police on this one there might come a time when they would be in a position to do her a favour in return. It would be a card she could keep up her sleeve as it were. Moreover, there was just an outside chance of a reward for information leading to an arrest. Alfred Baker had been a rich man and there would be money in the family. She had heard that there were two sons, and they would surely be grateful for any help in nailing the killer of their father.

So she got in touch with Detective Inspector Morton, and he came to see her at once at her flat; which was no great shakes in the accommodation line but suited her well enough.

Morton, of course, wanted to know why she had left it so long before reporting her discovery.

'Because I only just seen it, that's why. I was on a seat in Hyde Park and it just got sort of blown my way. Fate, I reckon.'

She did not tell him that this had happened some days ago. It was immaterial and she thought it might prejudice him against her. Besides annoying him.

Morton examined the picture and read the report. It was the first time he had seen either.

'You are sure this is the man you saw in Mr Baker's house?'

Miss Cant was reluctant to commit herself entirely. 'Well, nothing's certain, is it? I mean it could be his double, I suppose.'

Morton thought they could rule out the possibility of a double, but he still did not accept Miss Cant's identification as entirely reliable. She could be making a mistake. Nevertheless, it was a possible lead and he would certainly follow it up. The man in the photograph had not been named in the report, but the woman had and he could question her.

He thanked Miss Cant for her help. 'You did the right thing in bringing this to my notice.'

'I suppose,' she said, feeling the ground, 'there's been no reward offered? The family like.'

Morton smiled faintly. The idea of the Baker Brothers offering a reward amused him. But Miss Cant's words enlightened him regarding her motive in co-operating with the police. He had rather wondered about that.

'I'm afraid not, at the moment. But if anything of that sort should crop up I'll see to it that you are not forgotten.'

It was disappointing, but she had to accept it. She had little hope now that any cash would drift her way as the paper had. Fate was not as generous as that.

Morton lost no time in paying a visit to the Rag-Bag boutique in Chelsea. There he found Sharon and Kimberley and Jean Somers, but he could see that none of these looked at all like the woman in the photograph, who had been named as Rona Wickham.

He introduced himself and showed his warrant card and asked to have a word with Miss Somers in private. She raised no objection to this and conducted him to a cramped little office at the back of the shop where there was a desk littered with bits of paper and account books and some arty-crafty mugs with cold dregs of coffee in them. There were two hard chairs and a filing-cabinet and a word-processor, together with a pervading odour of stale cigarette smoke and perfume.

'Now, Inspector,' Miss Somers said, 'please tell me what this is all about.'

Morton took a wallet from his pocket and extracted from it the cutting from the *Comet* which Miss Cant had given him.

He showed it to Miss Somers, who of course had seen an exact replica of it some days earlier; though she did not say so.

'The lady in the photograph. It isn't you, is it?'

'Of course not. Surely you can see that. It's my partner, Rona Wickham. It says so there, doesn't it?'

'Just checking. Papers get things wrong, you know,' Morton said. He rather liked the look of Miss Somers. She was nicely made in a fairly solid kind of way, though certainly not what you could call fat, and she had a pleasant face and manner. He thought she would have been a jolly companion for an evening on the town and anything that might follow from that. But this had nothing to do with his purpose in being there, and he banished it from his mind. 'It was Miss Wickham I really wanted to see.'

'Why?' Miss Somers demanded. 'What's she done?'

'As far as I know she hasn't done anything. That is to say, nothing of a criminal nature.'

'Then why do you want to see her?'

'I'd like to speak to her.'

'About what?'

Morton felt that it was he who was being cross-examined, which was a complete reversal of the usual roles. However, he did not take offence. He simply answered mildly:

'About one of those gentlemen in the photograph.'

'Ah!' Miss Somers's reaction might have indicated that she had thought as much. 'I suppose you mean Martin. He's that one.' She pointed to the man in the picture who appeared to be knocking the other one to the floor. 'He's her current boyfriend. Though of course he's not exactly a boy, is he?'

'Martin?'

'Martin Keele,' Miss Somers said. And she was thinking how right she had been to have doubts about him. Because if the police were interested in him it had to mean that he was

151

a rotten apple, and she wondered just what he had done to warrant the attention of a detective inspector. So she asked. 'Why are you looking for him?'

'We think he may be able to assist us in our inquiries.'

'Oh!' she said. And she knew what that meant. It meant that he was jolly well guilty of something or other and they wanted to grill him about it.

'I wonder,' Morton said, 'whether you could give me his address?'

'Why, yes,' she said. And she dictated it to him while he jotted it down in his notebook.

And then she said: 'Are you thinking of paying a call on him?'

'That is my idea.'

'I'd forget about it if I were you.'

Morton looked surprised. 'Why do you say that?'

'Because you won't find him there. He and Rona have gone away for a long holiday. I don't know when they'll be back.'

Morton curbed an inclination to swear, and he managed to keep the note of exasperation out of his voice when he asked:

'Where have they gone?'

'I don't know. For some reason or other Martin wanted to keep it a secret. He hadn't even told her where they were going when they left. It would be abroad, of course.'

Morton reflected that he could have made a pretty shrewd guess at the reason why Keele had not wanted anyone to know where they were going, but he did not tell Miss Somers this. He just said:

'Well, in that case I suppose I shall just have to wait until they come back. And if you should get to hear of the address where they've gone to, you might let me know.'

He gave her the telephone number to ring, and she

152

promised to do as he had asked. She would be only too pleased to do it, because she was now very worried indeed about Rona. She figured that if a police officer like Morton was on Martin's tail the crime he was suspected of committing could hardly be a petty one. So there was Rona gone off nobody knew where with a man who could turn out to be a hardened criminal of the worst possible type. She had known all along that that lightning affair would turn out badly, and now she was being proved right.

If only she could have got in touch with Rona and warned her. But that was impossible.

Morton had a conference with Milburn and suggested that they should get a search warrant and go through Keele's house in Kensal Green with a fine-tooth comb.

'With what object?' Milburn inquired.

'We might pick up something that would help us.'

Milburn shook his head. 'Unlikely. He'll be too smart to leave anything incriminating lying around. And quite apart from that, there's not a hope we could get a warrant. What have we got? The word of a whore who thinks she recognises the killer in this photograph in the *Comet*. How much reliance can we put on that? You have to remember she gave a completely different description of him immediately after the crime had been committed. It doesn't fit the man in this picture at all. So there's confusion for you. Nothing really convincing to act on.'

'Suppose we were to bend the rules a bit. Go inside anyway and take a look round the place.'

Milburn raised his hands in mock horror. 'Frank, Frank! I don't believe what I'm hearing. You can't be serious. Suppose we broke in and found nothing to our purpose, and then it leaked out – as you can be sure it would. What a stink that would cause. Heads might roll, Frank, heads might roll.

No, it's just not on.'

Morton had reluctantly to agree. Milburn was right of course. But he felt more than ever frustrated. He had the name of his man now; he felt sure of it. And yet there was nothing he could do. Nothing but wait.

It made him furious.

Chapter Twenty
INFORMATION

Rona thought the bungalow was delightful. It was not very old and had been maintained in first-class order for the tourist trade. It had every convenience, and with just three bedrooms, two of which they were not using, it was not too big to be easily manageable with the help of the black woman, Sarah, who came in each morning to do the chores.

There was a verandah with cane chairs, where you could lounge at your ease and gaze out over the blue Caribbean Sea glinting in the sunlight, and watch the white sails of the boats or the occasional freighter or cruise liner passing by.

The bungalow was some two hundred yards from the water, a fairly steep track leading down to the smooth white sand of the cove; and one could not have asked for a more heavenly situation.

There were several more holiday homes scattered around, but none of them encroached too closely on any of the others, and there were coconut palms growing in the gaps between the buildings to give a certain amount of privacy.

A town was situated not far away along the coast, and there was a road leading to it on a meandering and rather switchback course. The name of the town was St Ann's, which was also the name of the island, and it was a bustling sort of place, with shops and street markets and an open-air cinema. Keele had rented a car and sometimes they would drive into town for shopping or entertainment, and once they had taken a trip completely round the island along the coastal road, with the sea always on the left and maybe a sheer cliff on one side and a long steep drop to the shore on the other.

Keele asked Rona whether she was not glad they had come to St Ann's.

'Oh yes,' she said. Though she had not known where they were going until they were on the plane, she did not mind now. It was all so splendid, and she admired him for making such a wonderful choice. 'I couldn't have asked for anything better. This is the best holiday I've ever had. You're a darling, Martin, you really are.'

He had been fortunate in getting the place at such short notice. By sheer good luck someone had made a last-minute cancellation no more than half an hour before he walked into the London agency. It was expensive of course; it was costing the earth; but it was worth it.

It was no use trying to kid himself, however, that he had found a permanent solution to his problem; he had merely bought himself a little time. The mouse had escaped into its hole, but it would eventually be forced to come out again. And the cat would be waiting.

But suppose he were never to go back? Suppose he were to stay permanently abroad? Not on this island necessarily. Brazil perhaps, where even the British police could never touch him. But had he enough money for that? It was doubtful. He was not a millionaire; he was a long way from that. And living in Brazil was fearfully expensive, so he had heard. And besides, would Rona agree to it? Would she not insist on going back home?

So was there an alternative? Yes, undoubtedly there was.

It was a dangerous one admittedly, but if anyone could manage it surely he was the man. He had the experience.

For the alternative was to return to England and remove the threat. Permanently. It would entail killing both the Baker Boys, and maybe Buster Jakes as well. It would not be easy, that was for sure; but it could be done. It had to be done.

It was, of course, not the way he had planned things. After the Alfred Baker job he had decided to give up the killing game once and for all. He was to have started a new life with Rona Wickham, leaving all that other business forever behind him. But fate had stepped in and had taken a hand in the matter in a way he could not have foreseen. So now he had to make new plans; he could not simply let things drift.

Some days they went sailing from the cove. Every day they swam in the warm clear-blue water. They lay in the sun and acquired a rich golden tan, using great quantities of protective lotion on their skin. He never tired of watching Rona in her scanty bikini.

'Do you know,' he said, 'what a voluptuous body you have?'

She laughed. 'Of course. Don't I see it in the glass?'

'But not with the eyes of a man.'

'And that makes a difference?'

'It makes all the difference,' he said. 'What should we do tomorrow?'

There was always a tomorrow; always something else to do. Life was very good.

One day she sent a card to Miss Somers. She did not tell Keele. It was when they were in St Ann's and had gone their separate ways for a time. She felt an urge to get in touch with her business partner, and she could see no harm now in letting her know where they were.

She did not realise that back in London quite a few people were showing an interest in the house in Kensal Green. There was no reason why she should have guessed that this was so, though Keele might not have been surprised.

One of the people was Buster Jakes. Under instructions from the Baker Boys he continued to stake out Keele's house with the purpose of giving the owner a worrying time of it. Jakes was none too quick on the uptake, and it took several days for him to suspect that Keele was no longer around and that all he was harassing was an empty house.

He passed on his suspicion to the Baker Boys. 'I think the bleeder's bin an' gone.'

'Wotcher mean, gone?' Barney demanded.

'What I say. Scarpered, taken a powder, legged it.'

'You sure?'

'No, I ain't sure. But I ain't sin 'im for a time now. I've rung the doorbell a few times an' got no answer.' Jakes suddenly became accusatory. 'I said we shoulda dealt with 'im when we 'ad the chance, but you wouldn't listen. You said to make 'im sweat for a bit. Well, he sweated all right; sweated hisself clean outa sight.'

'All right, all right!' Barney spoke sharply; not at all happy to be reminded of his own words. 'There's no harm done. He'll be back; he's bound to be. The house ain't up for sale, is it?'

'Ain't no sign up.'

'There you are then. Tell you what – me and Maurie'll go along an' take a look.'

'You won't find much,' Jakes said. He seemed determined to be gloomy about the prospects. 'It's like I said, the bleeder's gone.'

When the Baker Boys arrived at the house in Kensal Green it

seemed to them that Jakes could well have been right. They rang the doorbell but there was no sign of life within.

'Could just be out,' Maurice said. But he put forward the suggestion without much confidence, because after all Jakes had been hanging around the place for quite a while and had caught no glimpse of Keele. 'What do we do now? Wait?'

'No point in it.' Barney spoke disgustedly. 'That's what Buster's been doing. Be a waste of time. We've blown it, Maurie, we've bloody blown it.'

'But he'll be back eventually, won't he?'

'How do we know that? Just because there's no sale notice up don't prove he ain't gone for good. Maybe he only rented the place. Who knows? We was too bloody confident; we had to play a game with him, and now he's given us the slip.'

'It was your idea,' Maurice said.

'I didn't hear you raising any objection to it.'

'Well, no, but—'

'You blamin' me, Maurie?'

'No, I ain't blamin' you,' Maurice said.

But he was. In his mind he was. He had to blame someone, and it was certainly Barney who had suggested the cat-and-mouse lark. So who else was to blame?

A week passed, then another week. They continued to visit the house off and on to make sure there was still no one at home; and one day they were turning away from the door when they saw a man standing on the pavement and looking at them.

'You won't find anyone at home,' the man said. 'Mr Keele went away weeks ago.'

'You know Mr Keele then?' Barney said.

'Nodding acquaintance. Pass the time of day. Neighbours.

Never real close. Not an easy man to get close to.'

Barney felt that he would have gone along with that, for the present at least.

'You wouldn't happen to know where he's gone, I suppose?'

'Sorry, no. Holiday, I expect. Saw him carrying his bags out to a taxi. Him and his lady friend.'

'So he has a lady friend?'

'Oh yes. Name of Wickham. She's partner in that Chelsea boutique, the Rag-Bag. There was a piece in one of the papers not long ago when she and him had a bit of a dust-up with another guy in a West End bar. Maybe you saw it?'

'No,' Barney said. 'Must've missed that.'

'Well, you can't read them all, can you?'

When the man had departed the Baker Boys went back to their car and it took them no time at all to decide that their next move had to be a visit to the Rag-Bag. When they eventually found the place Barney stayed in the car while Maurice went inside to do the talking, because he was the handsome one and had the kind of charm that helped when you were trying to get information from a woman.

He asked to speak to the proprietress. Miss Somers came forward and took him into the office where he introduced himself as Arthur Green.

'I believe,' he said, 'you have a partner named Wickham.'

'Rona Wickham. Yes, that's so.'

'And she's presently on holiday with a Mr Martin Keele. Is that correct?'

'Yes. I told the inspector that, you know.'

'You told the inspector?' Maurice Baker's brain was racing to absorb this piece of information. It was apparent to him from what the woman had said that the police had already been to the Rag-Bag making inquiries about Keele; so they must have got on to him somehow. And now Miss Somers had jumped to the conclusion that he was a copper too, and he had to decide whether or not it would be to his advantage to play along with that idea. It took him no more than a moment to decide that it would. 'Oh, but of course you did. What am I thinking about?'

And then Miss Somers saved him the bother of thinking how to go on from there by saying: 'I'm so sorry. I promised to get in touch as soon as I had the address, but we've been so busy and it slipped my mind. But now you're here and I can give it to you, can't I?'

Maurice turned on his most charming smile and said: 'Yes, you can.'

'Are you an inspector too?'

'I'm afraid not,' Maurice said. 'Just a detective constable for the present.'

'Oh well. I'm sure you'll soon be promoted. You look very competent.'

'Nice of you to say so, ma'am.'

She went to the desk and fished a picture postcard out of a cubby-hole, and Maurice could see that the photograph on it was of a tropical beach with palm-trees in the background. Miss Somers found a slip of paper and copied the address with a ball-point pen. Then she handed the slip to Maurice.

'I hope I'm doing the right thing,' she said. 'But if he's done nothing wrong he has nothing to fear, has he? And if he has done something, well, it's only right you should know where he is, isn't it?'

Maurice agreed with her that it was. He thanked her for her co-operation and left the boutique.

When he got into the car Barney said: 'Well?'

'Yeah,' Maurice said.

'You got it?'

'I got it.'

'So where's the bastard gone?'

'The West Indies.'

'Oh my!' Barney said. 'An island in the sun. Better get out the tropical gear and the dark glasses.'

Chapter Twenty-One
RAT IN A TRAP

Keele had been down into St Ann's to buy a few stores – some bottles of wine, fruit and bread. Rona had decided not to accompany him, and he had left her reclining on one of the cane loungers on the verandah reading a paperback novel in which she had become engrossed.

It was pretty late in the afternoon when he drove back to the bungalow, and as he approached it he caught sight of a car he had not seen before parked a short distance further up the road. He thought nothing of it; it had probably been left there by somebody visiting one of the other bungalows or maybe going down to the beach.

He drove the rented Mondeo on to the shingle at the side of his own place, and he could see no one on the verandah, though the paperback that Rona had been reading was lying on the boards as though she had just dropped it there before going inside.

He went in by the back door, which opened into the kitchen, and he dumped the bottles and the polythene bags he had brought in on the table. He had rather expected Rona to be there, maybe preparing things for the evening meal, but she was not, and he could hear no sound of any movement inside the bungalow. This seemed odd. She would surely have heard the car drive up on to the shingle, and the natural thing would have been for her to come and see what he had brought back from St Ann's, or at least to call out a greeting to him. But the whole place was silent, apart from the low hum of the refrigerator.

A slight feeling of unease came over him, and he called out: 'Rona! Are you there?'

There was no answer, and his uneasiness increased. She might perhaps have gone down to the beach, but it seemed unlikely at this time of day, and she had never gone swimming except in his company. So where could she be?

He went into the passageway and opened the door on the right which gave access to the sitting-room, and he saw her at once, though the light in there was subdued by reason of the venetian blinds having been lowered over the windows. She was sitting on a chair facing the door, and her wrists were tied with cord and she had been gagged with a piece of cloth.

Sitting on another chair, dressed in a smart pearl-grey tropical suit and looking very much at his ease was one of the Baker Boys. Keele believed it was the one called Maurice. He had a self-loading pistol in his hand, but he was not pointing it at anybody; he was resting it negligently on his knee.

'Why don't you come right in?' he said. 'Make yourself at home, Mr Keele.'

Keele had come to an abrupt stop in the doorway. His instinct was to turn and get to hell out of there before Maurice Baker had time to lift the gun off his knee and let fly with it in his direction. But before he could even begin to move he heard a sound behind him, and something hard and cold was pressing into the nape of his neck and he had no need to be told that it was the lethal end of a pistol or revolver barrel.

A voice said: 'Don't do anything stupid.' And it was one he had heard before coming from a man sitting in a BMW car outside his house in Kensal Green. It was the voice of the elder Baker Boy, the one called Barney.

Barney said: 'I could blow a hole through the back of your skull if I felt like it.'

Keele sincerely hoped he would not feel like it. And apparently he did not – for the present at least. The cold metal shifted away from his neck and he was aware of Barney's hand doing a quick but thorough frisking job on him.

'It's okay,' he said, apparently addressing his brother. 'He ain't got nothing on him.'

As Keele was dressed in nothing but shorts and a bush jacket, apart from his shoes, it would have been difficult for him to conceal much in the way of armament upon his person, but the Bakers obviously believed in taking no chances. He wondered just how they had managed to get their guns, since they could not have brought them from London; airline security would have prevented that. But in St Ann's it was probably almost as easy to buy a gun as it was to order a meal in a restaurant; so no doubt they had picked up the weapons soon after arrival.

But how the devil had they got on to him? Nobody in London knew where he was. Or did they? He glanced at Rona, who was looking dead scared; which she had every right to be. But it must have been she who had brought this trouble on the two of them; he had no doubt whatever on that point, because she had been the only one besides himself who knew they were in St Ann's. Nothing could have been found out from the travel firm even if inquiries had been made, since he had used a false name when booking the holiday and the flight. And he himself had told no one, so it had to be her. She must have sent a letter or a card to that partner of hers at the Rag-Bag, and Miss Somers had blabbed; that was how it had to be.

But why would she have done so to the Baker Boys? Why not to the police, if to anyone? He could think of no answer to that one. And there was no time to give more thought to it just then, because when Barney had finished the frisking he told him to move over to the opposite side of the room and sit on a settee that was pushed up against the wall where they could keep an eye on him.

Keele could see now that the gun which Barney had been sticking into the nape of his neck was a magnum revolver, which would certainly have made an unholy mess of his cranium if the trigger had been squeezed, and it might also have spattered the other two persons in the room with his blood and brains at the same time. Which was perhaps one of the reasons why Barney had not done the shooting. It was probably not in the plan either; and he had no doubt they had a plan. But whatever it was, he guessed the ending was going to amount to much the same thing, and he was not going to like it.

Unless he could alter the programme. And at the moment it would have been very difficult indeed to convince himself that the Baker Boys did not have the better hand. In fact they might well have been said to hold all the aces in the pack.

All he could hope for was to find the joker. And that might take quite a bit of doing.

Barney stuck the magnum revolver in his belt and untied the gag that had been keeping Rona silent. He also released her hands. Then he sat down close to his brother who was still holding the self-loading pistol.

Maurice grinned at Rona. 'Sorry we had to do that. But we couldn't have you screaming your head off and warning the boyfriend when he walked in. You ain't gonna scream now, are you? I mean what good would it do? No close neighbours to come running to the rescue even if they was willing to. Which is doubtful.'

'What do you want?' she asked in a trembling voice. 'Who are you?'

'Oh, I forgot you didn't know. Pardon me for not introducing myself. I'm Maurice Baker and that there's my brother Barney.'

The surname seemed to touch a chord in her memory. 'Baker! Wasn't there someone of that name murdered in London not long ago?'

'Right in one, lady. Alfred Baker was our father. And that guy over there was the one what killed him.' His left forefinger shot out as though stabbing a hole in the air to point in accusation at Keele. 'Drilled him clean through the bean while he was lying in bed.'

She turned her head and stared at Keele. 'It's not true. It can't be true. You didn't, did you?'

Keele answered coolly: 'Yes, of course I did.'

'Oh, my God!' she said. 'Oh, my God!'

'So now you know why we're here,' Maurice said. 'To administer retribution, if you'll pardon the long words. To take our bloody revenge if you like that better. Took us a bit of time to get to him. Had to top a few others along the way. But now we're here and we've got him cornered like –'

'A rat in a trap? Is that the expression you were searching for?' Keele asked, sneering. He was still cool, ice-cool, though it was a warm afternoon that was now drifting into early evening. In a situation like this he seemed to forget the threat to his life, almost to take a perverse kind of pleasure in pitting his wits and his expertise against the opposition. He spoke to Miss Wickham. 'I suppose you wrote to your Rag-Bag colleague? I told you not to.'

'I know. But I didn't see any harm in it. I didn't know –'

'Didn't know he was a killer?' Barney said. 'No, I don't

suppose he would tell you that. Might spoil the romance. And it's not a matter of just the one, you know. Not for our Mr Keele. He's got a string of 'em to his name. Notches on the gun butt, you might say. It's his profession, you see. A contract killer. Does it for the money. Probably didn't know our old dad from Adam until he planted the lead between the eyeballs.'

She was staring at Barney in horror. And then her gaze shifted to Keele and she shuddered. Again she breathed, as if pleading for a repudiation of the charge:

'It isn't true. Say it's not true.'

And again he offered her no denial, nothing to ease the pain, not a grain of encouragement for her disbelief.

'It's true.'

Her head drooped. She could not bear to look at him any longer. It was as if the mere sight of him made her sick.

Keele spoke to Barney. 'So what happens now?'

'We wait.'

'What for?'

'It'll be dark soon.'

'You like to work in the dark?'

'Some jobs are best done then. You should know that.'

So they waited, and evening came with the darkness, and they switched on the light, the venetian blinds ensuring that no one could look in.

Barney suggested that they should have some refreshment, and he went with Rona to the kitchen and watched her while she made sandwiches and coffee.

'What made you take up with that guy?' he asked.

'I fell in love with him,' she said. She was calm now; the initial shock had passed, giving way to a kind of numbness. 'It was as simple as that.'

'And now? Are you still in love with him?'

She looked at him and seemed to be turning the question over in her mind. Then: 'It doesn't end in a moment, you know.'

He gave a grin. 'No, I don't know. I don't know a damn thing about that.'

In the sitting-room Maurice was saying: 'I'm surprised at you, Martin. I'd've expected a guy like you to have more sense than to get hisself hooked up with a dame, permanent like. They're poison. Can't trust 'em an inch. It was a weakness in you. And see what it leads to.'

'We all have weaknesses,' Keele said. And he watched Maurice, hawklike, weighing the chances of rushing him, getting to him before he had time to lift the gun and fire.

And Maurice guessed what he was thinking, and gave a laugh and said: 'Don't try it, mate. You'd get a bullet in the guts, and think what a mess that would make.'

'Why should I care? You're going to kill me anyway.'

'Yes, but while there's life there's hope. Ain't that what they say?'

'They say a lot of things, and half of them are not true. Fact is, I never did find out who they are.'

Rona brought the refreshment in on a tray with Barney Baker following her in. When they had finished she took away the plates and the coffee-cups and washed them up and put them away, while the man watched her with amusement.

'Like to keep things neat and tidy, do you?'

'Why shouldn't I?'

'Why not, if you like it that way? But it's all going to be for somebody else, ain't it?'

She did not ask him what he meant by that. She knew. And the knowledge brought a chill to her blood.

Chapter Twenty-Two
THE JOKER

It was very late when they left the bungalow, getting on towards two in the morning. The sky was cloudless, star-bright, with just a slice of moon. There was a light breeze coming off the sea to temper the warmth that had built up during the day.

Maurice was staying close to Keele and the pistol was in his hand. Keele might have made a run for it, but he knew that a bullet would have been in him before he had taken two paces. Barney had a hand on the woman's arm and he had warned her to behave.

'We're just going for a little ride. It's a nice night for it.'

They got on to the road and turned left and walked to where the car that Keele had seen earlier was parked. It was a red Nissan that had obviously been rented by the Baker Boys. Barney unlocked it and told Rona to get into the front passenger seat. When she hesitated he twisted her arm with a sudden viciousness that made her utter a cry of pain.

'Now get in.'

She did so and sat down, but did not fix the seat-belt, for where was the point? If you were going to be killed anyway.

Maurice jabbed Keele with the gun. 'Now you.'

Keele climbed into the back and Maurice sat beside him,

the gun still in his right hand. Keele was on his left and would have had to reach across him to get at the weapon. Barney had the revolver stuck in his belt while he drove. The woman could not have got it even if she had tried. She had no thought of trying. She had never handled a gun of any sort in her life.

The road went uphill for a short distance, then levelled out. There was scarcely any other traffic.

'Where are we going?' Keele asked.

'To the place,' Maurice said.

'What place would that be?'

'The place where it happens.'

Keele did not ask what would happen at the place. He knew. The cards were still being dealt and he could see no sign of the joker. Maybe it had been taken out of the pack.

They drove for about three miles along the scenic road and came to a point where it had climbed high above the sea which lay on the right. Here there was a parking place of about the size of a football pitch, where in daytime people stopped to picnic and admire the view. There were no cars there now, just bare dirt rammed down hard.

There was a low stone wall or parapet built in a rough semi-circle to enclose the parking place. On the other side of the parapet there was sheer cliff, with the sea maybe a hundred feet or more below washing at its foot. The slice of moon gave a faint silvery illumination to the scene when Barney had switched off the lights of the car.

'Now,' he said, 'we all get out.'

'Why?' Keele asked. 'Why not shoot us in here? Be nicer sitting down.'

'You ain't that stupid,' Barney said. 'You think we wanter take the car back covered in blood and bullet-holes? You think they wouldn't notice a little thing like that?'

'I can see it might cause some remark.'

'So let's get out.'

They all got out. Maurice stayed close to Keele, gun in hand. Barney was holding Rona's arm again, but the revolver was still stuck in his belt. He was wearing no jacket and the butt was visible in the moonlight.

'We found this place,' Barney said, 'when we was driving around looking for a suitable spot for an execution. It's ideal. Easy to dispose of the dead bodies, don't you see? Let's show them, Maurice, shall we?'

'Okay,' Maurice said. 'Come on. This way.'

They all walked to the parapet.

'Look down there,' Barney said.

Keele glanced down for a moment and saw the glimmer of white foam where the small waves were hitting the cliff. But the moment was a fleeting one, because suddenly he knew that the joker had come up and it was his card. It had left its appearance late, but not too late. Just like a joker to keep you guessing, keep you on your toes, waiting until the critical moment and then jumping up and grinning at you.

Maurice was on his right and for that one moment his attention had wandered and he had lowered the pistol. Barney was between Keele and the woman, and the butt of the revolver was sticking up within easy reach. Keele grabbed it, turned and shot Maurice in the chest.

Maurice had just time to fire one shot with the pistol, and Keele felt the bullet fan his cheek in passing. It was a close call, but the luck was running his way. He had the joker.

Barney had released his grip on the woman's arm, and he took a swing at Keele and knocked him down and fell on him. Keele was half-stunned and winded, but he still had the big magnum revolver in his hand. Barney made a grab at his wrist but could not hold it. Keele brought the gun round and shot him in the throat, and the blood spurted. He shoved the man away from him and stood up, legs a bit wobbly, head a bit muzzy; but nothing much wrong really, nothing at all.

Maurice was lying on his back, but he was not dead; he was even making an attempt to get up, though he had dropped the pistol. Keele stood over him and grinned at him.

'Goodbye, Maurie,' he said. 'Been nice knowing you.'

He levelled the revolver and shot him in the head. Then he turned and did the same to Barney, just to make sure. When he had done this he threw the revolver over the parapet into the sea.

He looked at Rona. She had shrunk away from that bloody scene and was staring in a kind of horrified stupor at the dead bodies.

'Are you okay?' he asked.

She said in a low shaking voice: 'You killed them.'

'Why, yes. It was either them or us. They wouldn't have spared you, you, know. They wouldn't have dared to. Me, they would have killed for revenge, you for insurance. That's the way it goes.'

She said nothing. He could see that she was trembling, but she would have to snap out of it, because there were things to do and he needed her help.

'We've got to get rid of them,' he said. 'Lend me a hand.'

'What are you going to do with them?'

'What they meant to do with us. Pitch them into the sea.'

But he could not persuade her to go near the bodies. She would not touch them. So he had to do it alone. It was harder, but not too hard. One after the other he dragged them to the parapet, lifted them over and tipped them into the sea that was seething far below.

The car was rather more of a problem, but he found a place where the parapet had begun to crumble, and he was able to kick some of it away to make a gap wide enough for the car to go through. It was pointed in the right direction and there was a slight downward slope. He released the handbrake and Rona had regained enough control over herself to help with the pushing. Once they had got it rolling it went like a dream. There was a bit of bumping as it went over the remains of the parapet, but then it was on its way. A chunk of cliff broke off at the edge and over it went.

He looked down and could see no sign of it above the surface. The water was deep just there. No doubt it would be found eventually, but perhaps not for a while. And there would be nothing to connect him with it. It was not his rented car.

There was some blood on the ground, but he kicked dust over it and hoped it would not be noticed. He picked up Maurice's pistol and tossed it into the sea to keep the revolver company.

'Now,' he said, 'we've got a long walk ahead of us, so we'd better make a start.'

Whenever they saw headlights approaching they got off the road out of sight; it was no time for hitch-hiking. But there were very few vehicles. One lorry had gone past while they were at the parking place, but the lights had not picked them up and it had not stopped.

They were back at the bungalow in less than an hour. When they were inside with the light on Keele could see what a state he was in. There was blood on his face and his hands and his clothes. Rona looked at him and put a hand to her mouth, her eyes widening.

'Oh my God! Just look at you!'

'Don't let it bother you,' he said. 'It's only blood and it's not mine and it's not yours. It could have been, but the joker came up. I hoped he would, though I couldn't see how, but he did. They had all the aces but I had the joker, and that's what counts in the end.'

He was laughing; a savage kind of laughter, eyes

gleaming. He had a feeling of elation. He had won. The odds had been against him, long odds, but he had won nevertheless.

'I don't know what you're talking about,' she said.

'No? Well, it doesn't matter.'

He went to the bathroom and stripped off the bloodstained clothing and stuffed it into a polythene bag. Tomorrow he would take it out to sea in a hired boat and drop it overboard with a weight to make it sink. The sea would take anything you wanted to be rid of. It had been taking the waste and pollution of humanity for centuries without complaint, and one more bag of bloody clothes would be of no consequence whatever. It had swallowed far worse things than that.

He stood under the shower, soaping and scrubbing himself until he felt certain that not a trace of the blood remained on his skin. He dried himself and pulled on a pair of clean shorts and went into the kitchen where Rona was sitting with her elbows on the table, staring at the opposite wall. She had not stirred from that position since they had got back.

'Cheer up,' he said. 'It's all turned out well. No need to be down in the dumps. The time for that is past.'

'I don't understand how you can treat it so lightly,' she said. 'Doesn't what has happened have any effect on you?'

'You can bet your sweet life it does. Because it means I'm free. Nobody can touch me now. We can go back to England and start again. Because the police haven't got a thing on me. Not a damned thing.'

'And you'll go on killing people? For money.'

'Oh no. I've given that up. I finished with it when I met you. That's the kind of effect you had on me.'

'But you've just killed two more.'

'Only because it was necessary. In self-defence.'

'Don't you have any remorse for what you've done? Not just them but the others who were no threat to you. Innocent people.'

'Remorse?' He seemed to be considering the question. Then he said: 'You know something? People put far too high a value on human life. It's only a temporary state when all's said and done. Nobody lives for ever. So what are a few years more or less? They're neither here nor there.'

'But you did your utmost to hang on to your own life.'

'Of course. That's human nature.'

'I really don't understand you,' she said. 'I don't understand you at all.'

'Never mind the understanding. As long as you love me. That's what matters. And you do, don't you? In spite of everything.'

She took some time to answer that, as though it needed a lot of thinking over. Then she said: 'Yes, I do. I can't help it, but I do. Maybe when it comes down to it I'm just bad. Maybe I'm as bad as you are, God help me.'

He laughed. 'That's my gal. So let's drink to it.'

He took one of the bottles of wine he had bought in St Ann's and opened it and poured two glasses.

'To us,' he said.

'To us,' she repeated.

They drank and looked into each other's eyes. And in hers he saw a hint of something he could not quite figure out. Could it have been mockery?

Chapter Twenty-Three
HOMECOMING

They returned to England a week later.

There had been a bit of a stir in St Ann's before they left, because two English visitors had apparently vanished without trace. They had not returned to their holiday accommodation, though their luggage was still there, and the car which they had rented had not been taken back to the hire firm. The possibility that there might be any criminal connection with this disappearance was played down by the local police and the *Daily Herald*, the only newspaper with any worthwhile circulation on the island, because nobody wanted to say anything that might adversely affect the tourist trade on which the prosperity of St Ann's was so greatly dependent.

Returning his own rented car to the same firm which had supplied the Baker Boys with theirs, Keele mentioned the mysterious disappearance, and the young black who took the Mondeo in gave it as his opinion that the two tourists had simply driven off the road at some point and that the car and the bodies were lying at the bottom of a ravine hidden by jungle.

'Either that or in the sea.'

Keele agreed that it seemed probable. 'Some people are

very careless drivers. You don't think they could have been murdered?'

The man gave a high-pitched giggling laugh. 'What you talkin' 'bout, man? We don't have murder on this here island. We're all peaceful folks hereabouts.'

'And that,' Keele said, 'is just the way it should be.'

There was no one sitting in a car outside the house in Kensal Green when they got back. Keele had not expected there would be. That vigil would have become pointless as soon as it had been learned that he had gone away. And of course Buster Jakes would have been aware that the Baker Boys had departed for the West Indies to finish the job they had failed to complete in London.

The house had that unlived-in feel to it which seemed to come from any fairly lengthy absence of occupants. The air had a stale, rather fusty odour, not at all pleasant. It was a dull overcast day and the place had a gloomy aspect, contrasting sharply with the bungalow in St Ann's, which had been light and airy. For the first time since he had bought the house Keele felt a certain dislike for it.

Rona shivered suddenly.

'Are you cold?' he asked.

'A little. But it's more than that. I think it's this house. Is it my imagination or has it really become darker and gloomier since we went away? I used to think it was quite a cheerful place.'

'But not now?'

'No, not now.'

So she had felt it too. The thought came into his head that what had changed was not the house; it was they. Could it be that what had happened in St Ann's had had this effect on both of them? Had the killing of the Baker Boys killed something in them also? The joy of life perhaps?

180

But no; that was nonsense. In his case certainly; for wherein had this latest killing been any different from those of the past? Well, there had been a difference of course: it had been a double killing and she had been there to see it.

So was this what it had become for both of them – a phantom returning now in another country, in another place; a spectre that would haunt them both for the rest of their lives?

He refused to believe it. This was fantasy, sheer fantasy. There were no phantoms; there were no spectres. There was simply an old house which had grown cold and cheerless in their absence.

'We could always move,' he said.

She glanced at him. 'Move?'

'Sell this house and move to another part of London. It would have to be London, I suppose, because of the Rag-Bag. You wouldn't want to give that up?'

'No, I wouldn't want that. Even if I wished to, which I don't, it wouldn't be fair to Jean.'

The question of fairness to her partner in the boutique business was not as important to him as it appeared to be to her. He believed that Miss Somers did not care for him, felt a certain animosity towards him in fact. And he was not much taken with her either.

'Well,' he said, 'it's something to think about.'

'Yes, I suppose it is.'

She still had the flat in Chiswick of course. They could have moved in there. But it would not really have been big enough, and she was certainly not going to suggest it. Nor would she give it up just yet. It represented a kind of insurance for the future; it was somewhere she could retreat to if ever retreat became desirable – or even imperative.

They began to settle in. She started unpacking and Keele went away to get the boiler going so that there would be hot water. He turned some of the radiators on too, although it was still summer, and gradually the dankness went out of the house and it became more welcoming.

Rona put a call through to the Rag-Bag to tell Jean they were home.

'Oh how nice it is to hear your voice again. How are you?' she said.

'Fine, just fine.'

'It was a good honeymoon?'

Rona had almost forgotten that this was what it had been supposed to be. And it had been at first. It had been simply marvellous and she had been in heaven. But then the Bakers had turned up and the dream was shattered. She remembered how she had been on the verandah reading that novel which she had never finished and probably never would finish now. She had looked up as though sensing that she was no longer alone, and there they were, standing just where the shingle joined the road, motionless, looking at her.

Then they started walking towards the bungalow, and she remembered how their feet had crunched on the shingle, and suddenly she had felt afraid. They came up the wooden steps on to the verandah, and she sat up and dropped the book and said:

'Who are you? What do you want?'

The one she now knew was Barney Baker said: 'We want you, lady. Let's go inside.'

She had a feeling that they knew Martin was not there. Perhaps they had seen him in St Ann's. The man who had spoken was red-haired, freckled hard-looking. The other was darker and handsome, a Latin type.

'Who are you?' she said again, getting up from the lounger.

'Never mind that,' the red-haired one said. He gripped her

arm and propelled her towards the door of the bungalow.

The other one was closing up behind and she had to go. It did not even occur to her to scream for help. There was no one nearby. What did occur to her was that the men intended raping her. What else could they want?

When they had bound her wrists and gagged her they told her. Rape was not in their minds; they wanted Martin. They let down the venetian blinds and waited. It seemed like an age. She saw that they had guns. They showed them to her and she was terrified. She believed they were waiting to kill Martin, but she did not know why.

'Are you still there?' Miss Somers asked. 'You've gone all silent. I asked if you had a good honeymoon.'

'Yes,' she said, 'the honeymoon was great.'

She did not mention what had come after. That was something that could not be told – ever.

'And you're feeling the better for it?'

'Oh yes.'

Miss Somers must have detected a certain lack of conviction in the answer. She said: 'You don't sound very sure of it. I hope you haven't been overdoing things.'

'Of course not.'

Was getting yourself bound and gagged and carried off at gun-point with Martin to be shot and thrown into the sea overdoing things? And then watching Martin shoot two men and cast their bodies into that same sea and helping to push their car in after them; was that overdoing things? Perhaps, just a little. It was not the kind of experience you expected on a holiday in the West Indies. Or anywhere else, for that matter.

And she could not confide all this to anyone. She had to keep it securely locked away in her own brain, her own memory. It could drive her crazy but she still could not talk about it.

183

'And you and Martin? Everything fine between you?'

Miss Wickham knew what she was asking. Had they tired of each other? Had they had fights? Had she discovered in that month together that they were incompatible? Ah, if that had been all she had discovered!

'Did you think it might not be?'

Miss Somers lied smoothly: 'Certainly not. But things don't always turn out well, do they?' She did not add that she had rather hoped they would not, that she did not trust Martin, and why in hell were the police so interested in him anyway? That was not something to discuss on the telephone. 'Well, I'm so glad you're back.'

'How's the Rag-Bag? All going well?'

'We've managed.'

'I'll be in tomorrow then. Okay?'

'And I'll be expecting you,' Miss Somers said.

'Who've you been talking to?' Keele asked.

'Jean.'

'Checking up on the Rag-Bag?'

'Yes. And letting her know we're back.'

'I suppose the business hasn't crashed during your absence?'

His tone, in which she detected a faintly sneering quality, offended her. He had always shown a certain contempt for the boutique, as though in his estimation it were little more than a plaything with which it pleased her to pass the time. Yet it was far more than that; it was a thriving enterprise which she and Jean had built up from nothing. Perhaps that was what irked him: the thought that she had her own profitable business which made her quite independent of him.

'No,' she said, 'it hasn't crashed. It appears to have been getting along very well without me.'

'That must be rather disappointing for you; the knowledge that you're not indispensable.'

'Not at all. I should have been surprised if I had been. All the same, Jean will be glad to have me back. It'll take some of the load off her shoulders.'

'So when do you propose starting work?'

'Tomorrow. I assume you have no objection?' It was her turn to be a trifle satirical, but he appeared not to notice it.

'Me? Why should I?'

'You'll be able to amuse yourself without me?'

'I imagine so.'

There had been a certain edginess in this brief exchange of words, of which they had perhaps both been aware. It might have been a hint, a warning even, that everything might not in future run smoothly in this partnership that had been based on something so unpredictable as human passion.

Or it might have meant nothing at all.

Chapter Twenty-Four
DISGRUNTLED

When Miss Wickham had gone off to work at the Rag-Bag next morning Keele decided to have a work-out at George's Gym.

George welcomed him rather as a stray sheep returned to the fold. 'Nice to see you again, Mr Keele. Beginning to think you'd given us up.'

'I've been away,' Keele said.

'Oh yes? Holiday, was it?'

'Yes. West Indies.'

'Ah, very nice. Never managed to get out that way meself. Most other places in my time but not the Americas. What they used to call the New World, ain't it?'

'So I believe.'

'Not so new now of course. Though geologically speaking I don't suppose it ever was any newer than the Old World, so to speak. Weather good?'

'Very good.'

'Yes, I reckon it would be. Always is out there. Except when there's a hurricane of course. You didn't get a hurricane?'

'No. Not the season for them.'

'Well, I must say you look the better for it. Nice suntan.'

Keele got away from George and changed his clothes and did some iron-pumping. But his heart was not in it. He felt depressed. What, he thought, did life hold for him now? He had no occupation, no friends, few ways of amusing himself.

There was Rona of course; he still had her; that at least was a consolation. Without her life would have been empty indeed.

And then it occurred to him that she held, if not his life, at least his liberty, in her hands. This was not a pleasing thought. Admittedly there was no threat from that quarter for the present; she loved him too deeply. But at some future date? Who could tell?

So had he not better be on the watch? For what? For any sign of a cooling in her attitude towards him? Maybe.

And if he noticed anything that might be a pointer in this respect, what then? Remove the threat? Remove it in the one certain way removal could be accomplished? The way in which he was so practised an operator?

Well, fortunately it had not come to that yet, and maybe it never would. He hoped so. But he could not be certain. As he had once remarked to Barney Baker, nothing in this world was certain, except death.

Rona Wickham had a long talk at the Rag-Bag with Jean Somers, while Sharon and Kimberley attended to the customers. Miss Somers demanded a full account of the West Indian holiday, and Miss Wickham had to be very selective in her narration. She wondered what her partner would have said if she had described to her the confrontation that had culminated in the bloody killing of the Baker Boys and the flinging of their bodies into the sea. The best that could be said for that kind of experience was that it relieved the monotony; but she for her part would have preferred any amount of monotony to that.

Anyway, Jean would probably not have believed her if she had told that story; she would have thought it was just a piece of fantasy, for that was what it would have sounded like. But it had been no fantasy, and it had not been a nightmare either. You woke from nightmares, but there had been no awakening from that.

So she left out all the really exciting part of the story and spoke only of the sailing and the swimming and the sunbathing, of rides in the rented car, of the gorgeous scenery and bustling St Ann's and the friendly people.

And then again Jean asked, as she had asked on the phone: 'So everything went well between you and Martin?'

'Yes. I told you.'

'So you did. Well, that's all right then.' She paused, and then, as if she had suddenly remembered something, she said: 'By the way, have you heard anything from the police?'

Miss Wickham stared at her, and her nerves started jangling. 'The police! No. Why should we?'

'Well, not you exactly, but Martin.'

'But why should Martin hear anything from them?'

'I don't know. But a few days after you'd left a detective inspector named Morton was in here asking about him. Apparently it had something to do with that affair at Reagan's.'

'In what way?'

'I don't know that either. But he had this cutting from the *Comet* with the picture of you and Martin and Paul, and he wanted to know who Martin was and where he lived.'

'Did you give him the address?'

'Why yes. There wasn't any harm in that, was there?'

'No, I suppose not.'

'And then I told him it was no use looking for Martin there because you and he had gone away for a holiday and nobody had been told where to.'

'So this was before I wrote to you?'

'Yes, of course.'

'So if the police didn't know where we were, why did you think they might have been in touch?'

'Ah, but they did know later, didn't they?'

'Did they? How?'

'Because some time later another detective called in and I gave the St Ann's address to him.'

Miss Wickham's mind was racing and an idea had come into her head. She said: 'What was the name of this second detective?'

'Arthur Green. I asked him if he was an inspector too, like the other one, but he said no, he was only a detective constable. He was a very pleasant young man and quite good-looking.'

'Did he have black curly hair and a dark complexion? Sort of Italian look?'

'Why, yes. How on earth did you guess?'

'Maybe I'm psychic,' Miss Wickham said. But she was thinking that this explained how the Baker Boys had got to them, because it was a dead cert that the so-called Arthur Green had been no policeman but Maurice Baker. 'So you haven't been in touch with Inspector Morton again?'

'No. He had asked me to let him know if I heard from you, and I promised I would. But I forgot, and then this other policeman came in, so there was no need, was there?'

'I suppose not.'

'Anyway, what's it all about? What has Martin done?'

'He hasn't done anything.'

'Then why are they looking for him?'

'I don't know.'

'Well, would you like Morton's telephone number which he said I was to ring? Then if Martin feels like clearing things up he could give him a buzz.'

'Yes,' Miss Wickham said, 'that might be a good idea.'

The fact was that Detective Inspector Morton had put the Baker murder inquiry to one side for the present. There were other cases that were demanding his attention and the matter of Martin Keele had slipped from his mind. He was doubtful anyway whether it would lead to anything. He did not regard Miss Cant as a very reliable witness, and her statement that the man in the photograph taken in Reagan's Bar was the one who had locked her in the bathroom after the shooting of Alfred Baker had to be treated with a good deal of suspicion. It would have been hardly feasible to arrest Keele on that evidence alone, though he might well have been brought in for questioning.

But at the moment nothing was moving on that front, and the return of Keele to his Kensal Green house was not even known to the police.

Buster Jakes was another person who might have taken an interest in the return of Martin Keele and Miss Rona Wickham if he had known about it. And it would undoubtedly have surprised him greatly. He had heard nothing from the Baker Boys since their departure for the West Indies, but he had not expected to hear anything. They were not in the habit of sending picture postcards, especially to him; and to ring him up by transatlantic telephone would have been deemed an unwarrantable expense. There was no reason to keep Jakes up to date with information regarding their activities in the Caribbean, and he knew it. So it did not bother him.

It did occur to him, however, that they were spending rather a long time in that part of the world, and this surprised him a little, since he would have expected them to carry out their mission without delay and head straight back home again. But maybe they liked it out there and were enjoying the high life for a while longer. Anyway it was no skin off his nose. They could stay there as long as they liked for all he cared.

Miss Cant wondered just what the hell was going on; for as far as she could tell her fingering of the man in the *Comet* photograph had set no wheels turning. She had heard of no arrest being made and she had not been called upon to deliver her verdict on an identity parade.

She might as well not have bothered to show the cutting to Inspector Morton and tell him this was his man having a set-to in a bar, because he seemed to have done nothing about it. But that was coppers for you. They probably didn't believe her because she was what she was. Okay then, if that was the way they felt; but they might at least have let her know what was what, seeing that she was an injured party and bloody well had a right to know, for God's sake.

But no; she got nothing; just a load of dead bloody silence and not even a vote of thanks for doing her duty as an honest citizen. Which she was, say what you might.

Thus Miss Amanda Cant; an honest citizen maybe, but a disgruntled one certainly. And who could blame her?

Chapter Twenty-Five
CLEVER RONA

On the second day after their return from the West Indies Keele decided that he needed a new pair of shoes to replace those jettisoned in the sea off the coast of St Ann's. Rona had already left for the boutique, and he took the Jaguar out of the garage and drove up to the West End.

It was not until he got there that he realised he had left his wallet in a different jacket from the one he was wearing. There was only one thing for it: he would have to drive back to Kensal Green and get it, since it contained not only his ready cash but also his credit cards. Fuming, he turned the car and set off for home.

He noticed that there were one or two more cars parked in the street than there had been when he left, but he thought nothing of it; and not wishing to waste any more time he did not bother to lock the Jaguar but left the key in the ignition. He expected to be in the house only a minute and there was little likelihood that anyone would steal the car in that time.

In the event he was destined to be in the house rather more than a minute. He had run upstairs to fetch the wallet and was returning to the ground floor when he saw that in his brief absence the front door had opened and there were now four men, who were complete strangers to him, crowded into the entrance hall. Two of the men were uniformed police officers, while the other two were in plain clothes.

His immediate impulse was to turn and run back up the stairs; but he realised that it would be useless to do so. They would follow and corner him; he could not hope to escape.

He attempted to brazen it out, though seeing little hope in this expedient either.

'What is the meaning of this? What are you doing in my house?'

One of the plain-clothes men said: 'Mr Martin Keele?'

'Yes, that is my name.'

'I am Detective Inspector Morton.' He showed his warrant card, which Keele scarcely glanced at. He had no doubt that it was genuine. 'And this is Detective Sergeant Braintree.' Morton indicated the other man in plain clothes.

'All right,' Keele said. 'So what do you want? Why are you here?'

'We have a warrant to search this house,' Morton said.

He showed the document, and Keele did not bother to read it either. It was obvious that something had gone wrong. He had imagined himself safe, but he must have overlooked something; he could not think what. Now he was in a fix, a real fix, and he could see no way of getting out of it. It would take more than a joker in the pack this time.

He had to watch while they searched the house. They found the black leather jacket and the black trousers and the gloves. In themselves they were hardly incriminating, but he could tell that to the inspector they were significant.

'You wear these often?' Morton asked.

'Occasionally.'

'Special occasions, perhaps?'

Keele said nothing.

They discovered the safe. They had been bound to. It was

behind a picture in a wall in a small downstairs room which he used as a study.

It was locked of course. Morton asked him to open it.

'Do I have to?'

'I'm afraid you do,' Morton said. 'You aren't going to be obstinate, are you? It won't do you any good, you know.'

He knew this was the truth. He had the combination in his head and he opened the safe.

'Now,' Morton said, 'this does look interesting.'

The Smith and Wesson revolver was there; the silencer was there; the ammunition. They had all been left there during his absence in the West Indies, and this was the first time he had opened the safe since his return. There was quite a deal of money in banknotes also.

Morton said: 'Do you have a permit for that weapon?'

It would have been pointless to claim that he had, since he could not have produced it.

'No.'

'Dear me! That is an offence, you know.'

As if he did not know! But he knew also that it was a very minor one compared with that with which they would undoubtedly charge him. The forensic experts would examine the revolver and they would prove that it had been the weapon that had propelled the bullet into Alfred Baker's head. They would have kept that bullet for this very purpose; and the bullets that had killed other victims, all fired from that same gun.

They had him. Oh, they well and truly had him now. He knew it and they knew it. Morton did not gloat, but there was that in his manner which bespoke triumph. He had got his man and he had reason to feel elated.

It was the sergeant who recited the statutory caution. But even before he had completed it Keele made his break for freedom. The suddenness of it took them by surprise; until that moment he had appeared to be accepting the situation with resignation and they had perhaps been a trifle complacent, not as watchful as they might have been.

He was out of the room before Morton or the sergeant realised what he was doing. In the hall there was only one constable standing between him and the front door. He went straight at the man and hit him with his clenched fist with such ferocity that he staggered and almost fell. Before he could recover Keele had the door open and was running to his car.

There was no one to stop him and he was into the driving seat in a moment. The key was still in the ignition and the engine started at a touch. He heard shouting. They were coming out of the house, yelling at him to stop, waving their arms, furious that they should have allowed him to slip through their fingers.

But they could not stop him. He was away and giving the Jaguar its head. Soon it was moving fast and he was overtaking other vehicles, driving to the danger of the public most certainly, but not giving a damn about that if only he could get away.

In a very short time he had turned on to the Kilburn High Road, and soon he was on the Edgware Road and nothing seemed yet to be on his tail. He was exultant; he felt he could still beat them if the luck held. He would get clear of London and ditch the car somewhere and just disappear. He would change his name, change his appearance, start afresh. He could do it; he knew he could. He had always done what he set out to do.

He still did not know who had put them on to him, but he could guess, because there was only one person it could have been: the loving partner of his bed and board, the delightful companion of his holiday in the sun, the divine Miss Rona Wickham. He had suspected it might come to this in the end if he did not take action to ensure against it. But he had never dreamed that it would come so soon. And so he had left it too late and she had beaten him to it. Ah, she had fooled him there. Clever Rona!

He was going through Hendon when he heard the first police siren and knew that the chase was really on. He avoided the motorway and turned off on to the road to Finchley and then headed for Barnet. But the police were still hanging on and they would be phoning ahead and maybe setting up road-blocks, but so far there had been none. He swung off to the right before reaching Barnet for fear of getting snarled up in the traffic of the town. He was now heading towards Enfield, but again he changed direction and got himself on the road to Potter's Bar.

He could hear no sound of the police siren now, and a glance in the mirror revealed no sign of it behind, so he guessed it must have got hung up somewhere or just didn't have the speed to hang on. So maybe he had a respite now, and he went hammering through Potter's Bar and took a minor road to the right and then branched off to the left on to a country road which meandered between hedges and fields of corn and here and there a clump of trees.

He was still driving fast, though he felt that he had thrown off the pursuit, and he came to a bend and there was a tractor hauling a trailer loaded with bales of hay. The tractor had just come through a field gateway, and it and the trailer filled the entire width of the narrow road. Keele had no time to brake. The Jaguar hit the trailer and smashed its side. He had not been wearing the seat-belt and he was thrown forward by the impact. The steering-wheel crushed his ribs and his head struck the windscreen. The skull was crushed and Martin Keele as a living sensate being ceased to exist.

Chapter Twenty-Six
ODD THING

Rona Wickham was at the Rag-Bag when the police called at the house in Kensal Green. She was aware of what might happen there, since it was she who had set the wheels turning by putting through a telephone call to Detective Inspector Frank Morton and having a brief but crucial conversation with him. In the course of this conversation she gave the inspector certain facts regarding Keele which were of particular interest to the police.

Having attended to this matter by means of the telephone in the Rag-Bag office she returned to some paperwork which she had been busy with. Miss Somers came into the office two minutes later and said:

'You've done it?'

'Yes.'

She had confided to Jean the whole story of the affair in St Ann's and the revelations concerning Martin. She felt she had to tell someone. Miss Somers had of course been horrified, but had given her full support. She did not say that she had always had reservations about Keele and had warned Rona not to be too trusting of someone she knew so little about, but Miss Wickham guessed that this was in her mind.

'So now they'll be on to him?'

'I suppose so.'

'And how are you feeling?'

'Depressed.'

Indeed she felt no satisfaction with what she had done, though she had known she had to do it. The germ of the idea had been in her mind ever since she had recovered from the initial shock of learning that Keele was a murderer, and one who killed people for money. But she had dissembled. She sensed that her own life might depend on hiding her true feelings from her lover. For she did not doubt that he would not have hesitated to kill her if he had believed she might be a threat to himself.

'And in a way, guilty.'

'But there's no reason why you should feel either depressed or guilty,' Miss Somers assured her. 'He's the guilty one. Anything that happens to him he's brought entirely on himself.'

This was true of course, and it was ridiculous to feel that she had betrayed him. It was not as if she owed him anything. True, he had saved her life when the Baker Boys would have killed her. But he had only done that because he was saving his own life. Hers was just part of the package. And was it not he who had put her life in danger in the first place? Moreover, had he not deceived her from the outset? He had lied to her about himself, concealed the villainous side of his character and presented only the charming front. And it had been charming; she had fallen for it. She had really been in love with him for a time; right up to the moment when she had learnt the brutal truth about him. That had killed her love.

And had he been in love with her? Perhaps, in his way. But it would not have stopped him from killing her if he had realised what a threat she was to him. However much he might have loved her, he had always loved himself far better.

'Well, at least,' she said, 'I shall be able to concentrate on the business now.'

Miss Somers gave a smile. 'I can see you're recovering already. Now perhaps I shall be able to take a break myself. That was the agreement, wasn't it?'

'Of course. I haven't forgotten. And I just hope your holiday is as good as the first part of mine was.'

Miss Somers smiled again. 'As long as the last part of it isn't as bad as yours was, I shall be happy.'

Down on the Costa Brava Racquel and Shirley, the two girlfriends left behind by the Baker Boys, were beginning to wonder why they were hearing nothing from home. It was several weeks since the brothers had gone away, and not a word had come through from them in all that time.

But the girls were not worried; they had easily found alternative male company and were certainly not feeling bored. Eventually the money supply might peter out and they might even lose possession of the villa they were living in at present. Then they would have to pack their bags and go back to London to hustle for a living as best they could.

But as yet there had been nothing to warn them of the hard times that might be just around the corner, and blissful in their ignorance, they continued to enjoy the good things of life under the scorching Spanish sun.

When the Baker Boys failed to return from the West Indies and more time passed Buster Jakes began to wonder just what could be keeping them. But he still did not worry too much until he saw an item in the paper about a person named Martin Keele who had escaped from police custody and had ended up dead in a wrecked Jaguar car.

This made him begin to think very hard, and what he thought was that maybe Barney and Maurice never would be coming back from that Caribbean island. Because maybe they had found Mr Keele too hot to handle and had ended up dead themselves. He could have asked questions, but he did not, because it was said by some wisecracker once that all you got from asking questions around and about was a reputation for asking questions. And what good did that kind of reputation ever do anyone, except maybe the clever guys on the TV quiz shows?

And then it occurred to Jakes that with the Baker Boys out of the way and never likely to come back, there was no good reason why he should not carry on the business on his own account – especially as there was no longer any competition in the form of the Rackerman mob.

So he got busy again in the old routine, and one of his first victims was a man named Smith, who had a small corner shop selling all manner of goods and open all hours. Mr Smith paid up, but he was very resentful about buying protection from Buster Jakes when the only danger he seemed to be in was from that same Buster Jakes himself. So he decided to do something about it.

Jakes should have realised of course that there was a very great number of Smiths doing business in London. You had only to look in the Phone Book to find evidence of this. Moreover, quite a number of these Smiths were very rich and powerful men indeed.

Now one of these very rich Smiths was a fairly close relation of the Smith whom Jakes had milked for protection money, and this small shopkeeper complained of the matter to the rich Smith, who happened to be a firm believer in free trade and all that kind of thing.

Nobody of course could have said for certain whether or not it was a result of this complaint, but one evening when

Jakes was drinking a quiet pint of bitter in his favourite public house, leaning on the bar and not doing anyone the least bit of harm, some joker walked in, hauled a pistol from his pocket and shot him clean through the head.

Then this same joker put the gun back in his pocket, gave a little cough as though apologising to all those present for any inconvenience he might have caused and walked out again.

There were a lot of people in the bar at the time, and the odd thing was that not one of them had ever set eyes on the man before. At least they all said they had not when the police asked them.

Jakes might have known him, but he was saying nothing. He would never say anything again.

Miss Cant had given up all hope of receiving any reward for her part in the apprehension of the murderer of Mr Baker. Nor did she think that she would be recompensed for her loss of earnings on that fatal night. So she decided that it would be best to forget the whole sorry affair and carry on her business as usual, advertising her services in the time-honoured way by leaving cards with her number marked on them in various telephone boxes here and there.

She had learned one lesson, however; and this was that one should never go to the bathroom in a client's house in the middle of the night. You never could tell what might happen on the other side of the door.